D0967893

# TRESPASSERS WELCOME HERE

## Karen Karbo

A FIRESIDE BOOK
Published by Simon & Schuster Inc.
New York   London   Toronto
Sydney   Tokyo   Singapore

**Fireside**
Simon & Schuster Building
Rockefeller Center
1230 Avenue of the Americas
New York, New York 10020

First Fireside Edition, 1990
Published by arrangement with G. P. Putnam's Sons

FIRESIDE and colophon are registered trademarks
of Simon & Schuster Inc.

Manufactured in the United States of America

10   9   8   7   6   5   4   3   2   1   Pbk.

Library of Congress Cataloging in Publication Data
Karbo, Karen.
    Trespassers welcome here/Karen Karbo.— 1st Fireside ed.
        p.   cm.
    "A Fireside book."
    I. Title.
PS3561.A584T7    1990
813'.54—dc20                                                            89-26355
                                                                            CIP

ISBN 0-671-70024-3 Pbk.

The following stories have been published previously, some in slightly different form:
"The Palace of Marriage," *The Village Voice;* "Tackling English," *ZYZZYVA;* "Dis-
arming Big Mad," *The Massachusetts Review;* "Death by Browsing," *Other Voices;* "Lenin
Lives," *Quarterly West.*

For Kelley

*with special thanks to*
Sally Cotton Wofford

# THE PALACE OF MARRIAGE

## YUZ BOGOGA

No Soviet emigrates for any real reason. Okay, Solzhenitsyn, Sharansky. But they are movie stars of emigration. No usual émigré has their problems. Usual émigré leaves because one night he starts talking. He is drinking and he is sad. He is in bad news with his boss, let's say, or some friend has disappeared forever into psychiatric hospital. No American can understand such sadness. This man is a bathtub drain with bathwater swirling down it all at same time.

For my wife, Bella Bellinka, and me it was one February midnight. Heat and light vanished from our apartment without warning. Such cold is impossible to remember. In Los Angeles we do nothing but perspire and squint; heat and sunlight are ever present here, careless, competent, extravagant, like Americans.

But that February night we huddled in bed wearing every clothes we could get on. We boiled potatoes for our pockets and socks. I had a cold; tears of ice formed at end of my dripping nose. We drank and drank.

We talked until our throats hurt about what we wanted. A lot, it was, for people who had next to nothing. It started with heat, then bloomed into things fantastic. Bella wanted clothes, shoes, stockings, mascara, manicures, bedroom slippers, highball glasses, mail order catalogues, marzipan, super-absorbency Tampax, *Vogue*, a subscription to *Vogue*, a job at *Vogue*, things of which I had never even heard.

I wanted a garden of cactus and a baby. First American Bogoga. Ernest Bogoga. William Bogoga. F. Scott Bogoga.

Bellinka humored me. My wishes were few and simple. Harmless dreams. But we were so stirred up. We got going. Our breath turned hot and thawed two small patches on window above our bed. I mashed a few potatoes still in my back pocket. Now I realize this sudden passion was sparked by thoughts of possibilities, not love.

One thing leads to another. Is most cruel fact on earth. *A* is one thing, *B* is other thing. *Leads to* is part no one can see or name. No one can say, "I am now living *leads to*." *Leads to* is how whole world winds up at *B*, biggest sins and mistakes.

Suddenly I am making application for visas. I am sitting in offices, waiting for signatures. I even say I am Jew to emigrate. Jews then they were letting out. Can you imagine, saying you are Jew to get out of persecution? But there I am. I have become Bogogowicz.

Then we are on airplane, sixteen hours in Vienna, ten in New York, finally soft, hot laundromat air of Los Angeles, palm trees as tall as skyscrapers, going, going, going, ending way up in mustardy haze in tiny, disappointing cluster of half-dead fronds. Cars like stars, splattering galaxy of black asphalt streets. Fantastic.

Every morning our neighbor does things naked on her terrace. Yoga, toenail polishing, needlepoint. Today is leg shaving.

Our apartments mirror each other across narrow driveway. Both are second floor. She supposes her pots of bushy ferns, avocado plants, and camellias hide her. But no. She is betrayed; I am one who is hidden. From bedroom window I watch. I watch her pink plastic shaver sail up her shin, over her knee, and beyond.

At 6:30 A.M. every day I hear her sliding door open, close. Out of bed I stumble, fumbling, putting on my glasses. At night I leave our bedroom curtain open.

Early morning is only reasonable time in Los Angeles in September. After around nine o'clock wind comes. Wind is hot, dry, as though someone put entire city in clothes dryer. People get bloody noses. Houses in Hollywood Hills burst into flames for no apparent reason. Every day smells like campfire. At night, faces and car windshields are coated with thin layers of soot.

Our neighbor lifts her head, sniffs. Air is already brown-orange with smoke from fires burning all night. But now is pleasant. She enjoys herself. She squirts on shaving cream, whistles Chopin. She is our first American neighbor: happy, cultured, clean, her nipples dark and flat as the disks underneath our living room chairs. They are for prevention of dents on wall-to-wall carpet, these disks. My Bella Bellinka loves them. They always seem to be on sale somewhere, and she buys more than we will ever need. Same with air fresheners. All my clothes smell now like pine trees. I have not seen one pine tree since we left Soviet Union.

My wife, my sweet Bella Bellinka, is asleep. Only her back rising up and down says she is breathing and still alive. She sleeps flat on her face. This is to keep her hairstyle from mussing.

When we became émigrés, Bellinka's hair became art. Every Thursday afternoon now she returns home from a person named Roger, her head balancing a high, bright, curled, crisp tower of hair. It comes before me, her husband, and makes her wary on performing wifely duty. She is afraid I will damage her curls, despite my promises.

Real reason is not her hair, of course. I see her eyes glimmer at night while watching couples in love wrestle on television. Simple fact is I am ugly and I am old. Not age old, but life old. I am fifty-four, Soviet, bald, and nearly blind. All I want in life are cactuses for my terrace, and a son.

I stand ogling my neighbor long after my interest goes. My leg gets a cramp. I love my Bella Bellinka. I ogle only to make Bella jealous a little. I believe things might improve between us if, first thing she opens her light-gray eyes, she is faced with my interest in another woman.

Instead Bellinka is irritated. "Yuz, shame on you! People call police for this here!" She whips curtains closed, swats my arm. Her low stern voice recalls when she used to reprimand a dog we had in Moscow. This old dog was incontinent, and loved our only rug.

"She is there in plain sight!" I say. "I am still a

man. Don't dish me over the coals. Please, Bella Bel-linka, I beg of you!"

"Oh, Yuz." She goes into bathroom.

Outside, palm trees lining our street are shaken awake by burst of wind. It starts already. It is said this wind, known as Santa Ana, makes people crazy. The fronds creak and groan in unison. I have never heard a tidal wave, but this is what I imagine it sounds like.

Bella Semyonovna and I argue violently about silly things. Where to buy ice cubes trays. What is cable TV and do we need it. Which bus goes where. How to keep our apartment cooler. We avoid argu-ing about things upon which we truly disagree. We are afraid. Now we are in America, there is no rea-son for our marriage.

In Soviet Union we married for reasons of hous-ing. Bella I met only once. She was cousin of fellow worker at laboratory, willing to do anything for per-manent residency permit in Moscow. She was too talkative, overweight, provincial. As a man mostly from Moscow, my advantage was clear. Somehow I was taller than her then.

She always carried around a *Vogue* magazine she got on black market. It got rained on, snowed on so often it disintegrated. Bella wept, as though she had lost her eyesight. I found her odd, but beautiful. And I was forty-eight years old, never in love, with a twelve-by-nine-foot apartment in central Moscow I inherited from my grandfather.

When we met on steps of Palace of Marriage for ceremony, Bella didn't recognize me. She passed right by and tapped on shoulder of a much taller, much younger man. Corrected, she blushed, stran-gled her bouquet in embarrassment. I perspired,

over-forgave her. She asked how big was apartment
again. Thirteen by ten feet, I said, increasing the
measurements. I invented a large kitchen, in case
seeing me in cruel gray daylight changed her mind.

Accounting entered our young relationship there
and then. Yuz forgives; Bella is forgiven. Yuz has
Moscow apartment: Bella has nothing. Bella wants
to emigrate; Yuz loses good job in applying for visas.
Yuz wants a child; Bella falls asleep instantly. Bella
is forty. I know what is happening. She is waiting to
shift blame from herself to biology.

Yuz loves Bella; Bella tolerates Yuz, remembering all she owes him.

Every person who tries to emigrate loses his job,
first thing. I worked in special research laboratory
as operator of machine that washed and sterilized
laboratory instruments, petri dishes. This was special lab in dull green building, huge and unmarked,
on Kropotkin Street. It was place for researching
in-vitro fertilization.

My petri dishes grew humans. Or tried to. They
were old dishes, warped a little. They appeared to
seal properly, but actually allowed all kinds of things
to grow inside. Humans never got so far. There had
never been a baby from that place yet. Either egg
and sperm never got along, or women who came for
implantation had so many abortions that no embryo
could get foothold. Crude jokes went around.

Once, at end of my shift, near my last days there,
when all instruments and dishes were clean, slick
and steaming, I found incubator where special petri
dishes were kept. Light shining on them was yellow
warm. Culture medium was scab color, dishes looked
innocent, empty. But I knew, I knew. Here were
racks and racks of potential Soviet citizens. Dumb

cells being coaxed along for eventual implantation, birth, then what? Thirty years washing laboratory instruments for lucky ones.

I went home right away. Bella was packing her china, her most beloved thing. She thought she could take it with her, even though I tried to persuade her we would never be able to get it out.

I said, "If we ever get to America we must have child." Bellinka, so anxious to emigrate, so afraid it would not happen if she made trouble, promised me yes. She says now she only said she'd think about it.

But that cold dull day is scar on memory. The rusty red disks glowing under their artificial sun, the humble worried face of my wife, her nod. A cracked teacup in her hand. A baby, yes. Frank Bogoga. Don Bogoga. Brooke Bogoga.

I cook breakfast while Bella prepares to go to work. She is T.A., teaching assistant of beginning Russian at university. I do not know what this is, but I know she brings home paycheck and takes classes in Advanced Russian Syntax. Neither of us have ever heard of syntax before this job. It sounds like something to do with space.

I drop icy-hard waffles in toaster. Eggo, they are called. Syrup in babushka-shaped bottle. Instant Tang. I also open package of Sno Balls, chocolate cake with pink coconut-flavored foam outside. It seems to me all American food looks like it could be sold in toy stores.

I said this once to Claire Davis, secretary at Department of Slavic Languages, where Bella teaches. Her laugh was like bullets, Ha! Ha! Ha! She is making fun, or what? No, she said I was a stitch.

What it is, a stitch? Why is food funny? I never know if America is serious or joking.

Outside our kitchen window is something I will never understand. A billboard higher and bigger than any I ever see. Is several blocks away, looming over all smaller buildings between us. On it is redheaded girl in sunglasses standing, one hip jutted out. She has tight, fierce green pants, breasts the size of hot-air balloons floating up under black T-shirt. This is all, except TEENA spelled in big glittery plates that reflect sunlight. In middle of night I come into kitchen for water, and she is there. Lights from bottom of billboard shine on her all twenty-four hours. Through our thin curtains her legs look like two green smokestacks colliding. Who she is? Does she advertise a movie, beer, car telephones?

Bella scuttles in, sandals in hand. "What does Teena advertise?" I ask.

On television, my regular morning program is interrupted to tell what areas of Los Angeles are in danger of brush fires. People are told to water down their roofs. This is like watering down drinks? So much is confusing. Waffles are burnt around edges, still frozen in center. Morning program resumes. A dog psychologist is being interviewed. He says the dog has really got to want to change.

Bella laughs. "Teena is fantastic."

"What it is for, Teena? She actress?" I make a butter sandwich of my Eggos. I like my Tang straight from jar with no water added.

"Who knows. Not so much butter, Yuz. Bad for heart."

"How can she be fantastic if you do not know what she is? Is wasteful, all that paint. She is fantastic and no one knows what she is for? Is ridiculous."

"No," says Bella. "You are ridiculous. She is pretty, that's all. Please just to go with it, okay?"

"*Go* with it? What is that? With what am I supposed to go? You copy Americans like a big talking Russian bird."

"You are hopeless," she says. "I am not big." She pushes her waffle aside, begins applying her makeup. She does this at breakfast table so to have benefit of natural daylight. All her ladies' fashion magazines say makeup is best applied this way, in this light, and so she does. She is slave of those magazines.

I stare at her. To her I am like a television channel changed. She is not angry, or even flustered. She sips coffee from one of her china cups. She dragged them through after all. They are cheap, homely white. When she opened carton, second day we arrived, all handles were broken off. Broken and stolen, for they were nowhere.

Bella Bellinka is like these cups. An empty one. Broken but still able to float. Floating upon America. She is tiny and fragile, the ocean immense, but she soars in the sunshine, up one tall wave, down another, never sinking. She goes with it. I know this expression. Never would I use it. We are not so American as she likes to imagine.

"Perhaps emigration was not right," I say. "Is so difficult in Los Angeles. So difficult for Yuz."

"Yuzushka, please. You have job. We both do. Soon we will have car. Is heat making you upset? I will make you more Eggos. But no butter! Promise Bella." She hurries around kitchen. She pours me more coffee, even though I have some.


My job is as photocopier. Los Angeles motto is no place you can walk to is worth working at, but is not true. Captain Copy is eleven blocks from our apartment. Is air-conditioned, decorated with pink fishing nets hung up, painted starfish with glitter. Free coffee on all day.

Today, as I walk, a red sun sits on my bald head. The sky is thick and yellow. I have my hat, but I will not wear it in public. Is a white sailor hat, with *Yooz Andreyevich* sewn in blue thread. Except owner, everyone at Captain Copy must wear these hats. The first one they gave me said *Use.* I made them do over. New one said *Yooz,* a clown name, even worse. Bogogas have dignity, I insisted. My name is Yuz. My heart slugged against my chest. They refused to try again. I forced them to add *Andreyevich.* They called me a stupid old pinko. What is that, a fish? Wind rolls an empty garbage can down middle of street against traffic. Cars swerve to miss it, but no one gets out to turn it right. My lips, they are so chapped.

I have one friend in Los Angeles. Pak, a square, wavy-haired Korean. He works at Captain Copy seven years. He has had three hats, all of them misspelled *Pack.* Most of our business is screenplays for movies. Fast rich people in shorts come in, jiggle their legs, their keys, while waiting.

When no one is there, we photocopy body parts. We read screenplays. Pak is teaching himself English this way. "CUT TO—Lunch" he says when he goes out at noon. "CUT TO—The Next Day," he says every morning.

We tell each other everything, but as with Americans, I don't understand all. Pak has problems with his car, he stole it or had it stolen. There is some tube situation also. Either inside his wife or the television set.

Today boss is on vacation in Mexico, someplace that starts with X. I sit by coffeemaker and eat spoonfuls of coffee whitener. I have somehow gotten on subject of cactus. Pak photocopies without putting down lid. Every few seconds a white flash bleaches his sallow face. I think he may go blind. I tell him. He nods and grins.

"I want garden, Pak. Is only matter of going, putting down two eighty-nine, taking my bunny ears, my baby toes or aloe, and starting, right? But what if I spend every moneys on powder puffs and silk pincushions, only to discover I want organ pipes and prickly pears? Too much choice. My wife says is typical Soviet fear."

"CAMERA ZOOMS IN ON YUZ," says Pak. "He is a burned-out shell of a man, but has quite a way with the ladies. Think young Burt Reynolds."

I make Pak sit down. I think perhaps hot Los Angeles wind dries his brain up.


Evening comes. Wind stays. Bella Semyonovna and I ride bus to Department of Slavic Languages for special get-together party. Invitation says we are gathering to welcome all new faculty and students. It takes forty-five minutes to go twelve miles from our apartment to university. Smells of urine, melting plastic bus seats. Bella complains her thighs are sticking. She has a new dress, new silver high-heel shoes.

We pass bank sign saying 6:30, temperature 101. A man at front of bus steals wallet from blind woman's purse. Her eye dog licks his shoe. People are desperate. Sky is blotted with sulfurous smoke. Fires wink in the hills. Like Russian steppes, Los Angeles sometimes seems emptied of weather. All clouds, rains, frosts, and fogs are scooped out, leaving only this monotonous wind. I say this to Bella. She shrugs: Is better than freezing rain. She is reading one of her magazines. "Make Your Lovemaking

Aerobically Efficient!" A picture shows two tan peo-
ple in bed wearing sweatbands and stopwatches.
"Huh," I say. "Why you reading that?"
She shuts magazine, pretends she hasn't heard.

Slavic Department is small and crowded. I drink
four or five vodkas just so I can speak. I am shy.
There are mostly professors, a few students. They
huddle in circles that keep breaking apart and re-
forming, the way low-level life forms reproduce.
They sweat, swab their suntan faces with their
hands.

Bella has propped me by food table, so she can
mingle. I eat hard-boiled eggs, their yolks suffocated
in black caviar. One after another I eat.

These people mean much to Bella. Her dimples
work overtime. I hear her across room, through
chinks in party noise, giggling and calling people
Cookie. She never says Cookie at home.

Claire Davis, secretary to Slavic Department,
arrives. She says she stopped for ice. She is tall.
Her face is like loud music. Freckles, moles, wild
eyebrows, green-gold-brown eyes, all going at once.
She is not Slavic. She says when she took this
job she thought Slavic was inventor of artificial
heart. She only works here because she wants to
write. She is illiterate, then, or what? She wants to
write Russian?

She reaches over and pinches my side. "How's
it going, Yuz?"

"Good, good," I mumble, my mouth full of egg.

She throws herself down in a folding chair. She
wears shorts. I am drunk. Her knees stare up at me.
Two doorknobs wrapped in silk, sprouting tender
blond hair. "Yuz, now that is a cool tie. It looks like
Las Vegas."

I look down. My tie is deep green, tiny saguaro cactus stitched on, stems bent like arms. I found it one day in Dumpster behind our apartment.

"I call it my cac-tie," I say.

"Ha! Ha! Ha!" Her bullet laugh. She loves this. She pulls over a tall, thin boy. His bony jaw chewing looks like machinery. He wears a T-shirt that says TOO MEAN TO MARRY. "Pencil Neck," she says to him, "check this out. It's his cac-tie."

"Boooooooo!" says Pencil Neck, but he laughs too.

People are interested. They stop by food table for crackers, more vodka, and stay to admire. They love that I found it among garbage. Jim Spaniel, assistant professor of Soviet Society and Culture, says he admires my audacity. I say I thought audacity was some medical procedure. I am going in for an audacity. People laugh. Claire refills my glass. You are *something*, she says.

Dr. Vera Omulchenko, department chairman, says, "Yuz, Bella never told us you were such a wit." She has arrived late, giving car trouble as reason. However, I notice she comes with Sergei Lublinsky, famous émigré writer. Lipstick is smeared around her lips, her eyes a little sleepy. Those lovers are around the age of Bella and me, I think.

"That tie is"—Sergei Lublinsky wags his finger at it, thinking—"camp."

"Camp? Only camp I know is where my father lived almost his whole life."

"Your father was in a concentration camp?" Claire's smile drops. She leans closer.

"Magnitogorsk. Labor camp. Fourteen years he lives on soup of rotten cabbage and garbage parts of animals. In deepest winter his shoes were scraps of rubber tied to his feet with wire. And what for?

Stealing food ration card from dead neighbor's body."

"You guys," says Claire. "I can't imagine. I have a trauma if I can't get a new outfit." She looks at me, waiting.

I go on. Vodka is caring; it numbs you before reopening all those deep old wounds. I speak to Claire's knees.

"My father was a thermostat. This is real. Commissar had greenhouse. Is built of cypress, greenhouse. These days all are plastic, but in Soviet Union in 1937 they are cypress. Each morning my father gets up to fire boiler for heating, takes care of opening and closing of ventilation. Imagine, at labor camp, tiny greenhouse of birds of paradise, hibiscus, camellias. No prisoner was to know of greenhouse. Those who found out disappeared.

"Once, there is no electricity. Greenhouse goes dark, cold, snow blows inside vents, things freeze. But succulents grow, even there, even then. They huddle near ground, keep all nourishment inside. Surviving is what they do.

"My father was a cactus himself. White hair out like so, fierce expression and tough skin, tough short barrel man. Like me, you know, only better eyesight and not so bald. He manages to get his clothes patched with newspapers so he can read up on latest propaganda. He even gets friend on women's side of camp. He never sees her face but finds loose board at back of compound near latrines. He can reach through, feel her slim ankles, her breasts. . . ." I have never talked so much to an American in my life. Waves of memories crash through my head.

"Hi, Cookies." Is Bella. She pats back of her hair. I realize no woman in this room has hair like hers. It looks like a dessert. "Has Yuz been folding your ear?"

Claire laughs. "Bending our ears. No, this stuff's great. I mean, awful. Incredible."

Bella looks at her a little icy. "Time to go," she says to me.

"A few minutes more," I say. "They like my tie."

"Yes? We purchase at downtown Bullock's department store. My friend Cricket, she is salesgirl of sportswear, instructed us. Is chic, you know."

Claire raises an eyebrow at Jim Spaniel. He has taken some notes on my story, on a tiny pad of paper with a tiny pencil. They begin to laugh. Is low, chugging laugh of people who are tired and hot. I join in. Laughter feeds laughter. We cannot stop.

Bella folds her arms, grows furious. "Yuz Andreyevich, you are laughing at me?"

"We are," I say.

I go home alone.

Claire gives me ride. Wide black streets are empty. The night smells charred. Another bank sign. Time 11:45, temperature still 101. I ask how can it be? Sign must be broken. Claire says she heard it was going to get hotter. She drifts from lane to lane. Driving by braille, she calls it. Braille part is when she bumps over reflective lane markers. Tonight she's had six vodkas and a peach. She says she's on a diet.

When we cross Wilshire Boulevard she says, "Just think, if you took this street all the way to the end you'd hit the ocean, then Japan, then Russia."

"My thinking is not so big," I say. "That is Bella's way of thinking. She loves looking out of airplane windows."

"Oh, yeah," says Claire. "You worked in a laboratory or something."

I told her how it was. How we failed at in-vitro. "Just like you put first man on moon," I say.

"*Us?* You mean Americans? Now you're us too."

"Is impossible," I say. I smile anyway.

Claire's car is air-conditioned. I lean my head against window. I have never driven alone in a car with an American. A fire truck speeds past, lights whirling but no siren. She tells me about woman she read about who was denied artificial insemination because she wanted a baby on her own. She hated men but loved babies. Claire says this woman used turkey baster. She got some guy who was willing, then impregnates herself. And it worked. Could I believe it?

"Sure," I say. "They have dog psychologists here." I roll down my window. Claire is too young, too foreign. Breathing, even in her air-conditioning, is like inhaling gauze.

We stop in front of my apartment building. I get out. "*Spasiba,* Claire. You are good girl. Say, I mean to ask. Who is this Teena?" I point to billboard. Giantess Teena leers down at us from nighttime sky. Her lips are pink and full. Merciless.

Claire doesn't even need to look. "Nobody. That's her thing."

"She is an actress, singer?"

"She's on billboards. It's a gimmick. You know what a gimmick is? She doesn't do anything. She's a personality."

"She is famous? For doing nothing?"

"Sort of. Yeah, I guess."

I know what is turkey baster. I know because Bella Bellinka went to garage sale down our street and bought an entire drawer of kitchen instruments for fifty cents. We have this drawer sitting on our kitchen counter. At bottom of it, under bottle openers, corkscrews, spatulas, and many other mysterious things, is decal of person named Barney Rubble. Bellinka and I planned to use turkey baster for our first Thanksgiving. But I will use it now. Robert Bogoga. Madonna Bogoga. Sly Bogoga. Garage sale was being given by a woman who was going to prison.

I fill turkey baster while leaning against kitchen counter.

I am drunk, sure, but what is that? I was forty-eight when I met Bella, and am a drinker since age thirteen. I am saying I have performed this very thing while drunk for many cold decades. I still have on my tie. My mind provides its old slide show. With one hand I push open kitchen curtain. Teena Teeninka, American saint of nobody and nothing, spurs me on.

The lights of Los Angeles reflect off its smoky, smoggy ceiling, giving our bedroom a murky glow. Bella is asleep on her back, her arms and legs tossed away from her. Heat has driven her to this. Curtains and windows are open. I sit on bed edge. The bulb of turkey baster is greasy. Our neighbor is having a party. Music, a fan whirring. Someone yells *Addis Ababa!* A few people applaud. Clark Kent Bogoga. James Bond Bogoga. I know I cannot stop. To stop is to think. Outside, wind has died, but still shrieks around inside my head.

I move Bella's leg.

Suddenly her eyes click open. "Yuz?"

I throw myself on her. She doesn't yell. She growls Russian curses. She smells of toothpaste, vodka, cheese. She grabs my ears. Her nightgown slides up. "How many eyes does an earthworm have?" says someone across the way.

My hands land on her hairdo. She pulls on my ears, kicks at my thighs.

"You filthy Cossack!" she screams. She hates me. She says I am stupid old man. I rub her curls flat. This is what I've wanted, I know it now, yes! They are stiff. They crackle at my touch.

Finally, I stop. I stand. My turkey baster and future progeny have rolled behind bed, to join their fate with lint and lost shoes.

"I am sorry," I say. Sweat blinds me. My shins ache.

"You are disgusting drunken stupid man," she says. She rubs her neck. "Claire is not impressed with you; she feels sorry for you. She listens to your stupid stories from pity."

"Bellinka, I am sorry."

"You are joke to them, those Americans."

"We both are," I say.

She is so stunned to hear this she nods. "Yes, but at least I know this! I have my feelers open. I am no stupid."

"Is so hot," I say.

And quiet, suddenly. Like many people holding their breath. I look out bedroom window. Our neighbor, standing on her terrace, among her jasmine and dwarf orange trees, watches. She is with a man and another couple. They hold wine goblets, bob their heads around to see. Behind them, in living room, colorful board game is laid out on coffee table. I try to imagine my wife with these tall, brown fun people; a thick, simple cactus lost among lilies.

"What you are looking at!" Bella moves behind me, crosses her arms over her chest.

One of the men asks us if everything is all right.

"They're Russian," my neighbor says.

"Oh. I didn't know."

"What, that explains it?" Bellinka says to him. "As though we are only people to do crazy things?"

"Los Angeles is to blame," I say.

From habit Bella pats her hair, even though it stands up like weeds.

I close the curtains.

# TACKLING ENGLISH

## VALERIA CHALISIAN

I dreamed I was having brain surgery. I was sitting
on the tall white stool in the kitchen of our apartment in Kiev, the one I used to sit on when Grandmother cut my hair. Only instead of Grandmother,
standing behind me was a surgeon wielding a needle-
thin, shock-producing probe. It was not gruesome; I
was bald and serene, like the patient in an ancient
pen-and-watercolor done by one of the fathers of
physiology. The top of my skull opened from a delicate gold hinge at the back of my head.

When I was studying to be a nurse at the No-
vember 17th Medical Institute of the Ukraine, I read
of an experiment on the brain of a bilingual person:
a probe producing shock to one part caused the patient to say "apple"; a shock to another part caused
the patient to utter "pomme."

The surgeon was applying the probe to search for my English. I was hopeful for him to find it.

Tonight, before the dream, I celebrated my thirty-third birthday with my husband, Pyotr, who brought me to Los Angeles from Kiev four months ago. I hinted around that I wanted a pair of those excellent Top-Sider shoes like Claire, the secretary in the Department of Slavic Languages, wears with her blue jeans, as do all the university girls. Instead he presented me with a Gluzinsky Russian-English dictionary. It weighs twelve pounds. I weighed it on the bathroom scale.

I have an English phrasebook I carry in my purse at all times, and a colloquial-English book in the top drawer of my desk at the office. My husband says I will never learn true English from these books. "They are for wimps, Valeria," he says.

What does he know from language books and wimps? I think. My husband speaks four languages: Russian, of course, and the German, Swedish, and English of comic books, television, and pornographic movies. I envy his lack of shame. He wraps gifts by stapling the top of the paper bag they arrive home in, and as I reached inside for the Gluzinsky, I received a pair of scratches, a long red 11, from the pointy legs of a staple.

He swept aside our plates of untouched birthday cake with the side of his arm, intent on showing me the wonders of the Gluzinsky.

"Look. Under the word 'a' alone there is 'He doesn't know A from B'; 'He knows it from A to Z'; 'A-line dress'; 'A-bomb'; 'It's as simple as ABC.' Now you will have American at your fingertips, Valeria."

I nodded my head and smiled. I arranged my face to look as though I was capable of commenting but was just in a quiet mood.

"Say it," he urged. He never believes my face.

Why does he do this to me? He knows I understand most of what he says. I nibbled at a strip of skin already chewed raw next to my thumbnail. Whenever anyone speaks English at me, I feel as though they've opened a hole in the sole of my foot, and all the blood is rushing out of my body. I told this to him once, and he said, "That explains your stage fright, Valeria, but does not excuse it."

The brain surgery dream was awful and endless. It was like running uphill in slow motion, me on the stool, waiting for English to leap from my mouth. Finally, the surgeon pronounced: "Strange. This woman has no language at all." I tried to plead, "Where is my Russian?" but the dream unraveled there.

My husband is asleep next to me, and next to him, on the floor on her red plaid pillow, is Catherine the Great, our Scottish terrier. One of them is snoring. I get out of bed and crawl into my bathrobe.

In the kitchen, the dirty dishes from my birthday celebration have been placed in jumbled stacks on one side of the table; on the other, centered authoritatively on my place mat, is the Gluzinsky. My husband must have arranged this while he was letting Catherine the Great out for the last time. His job in Kiev involved deciding which slogans should be painted on which buildings for maximum exposure and inspiration. For example, "Long Live the Great and Good Motherland" on the side of the Palace of Marriage. He often uses this skill for my own instruction.

I sit down at the table and flip open the book. I see the word "big," under which appears "That's big of you!" I look up "so" and see that there is also a "so-so." I think of when my husband makes love to me and mutters, "So so so so beautiful." Is he saying four "so"s or two "so-so"s?

I cannot look up the only phrase I am eager to know. I have a feeling that if it isn't here, then I will never know what it means. The surgeon of my dream couldn't locate my English, and I won't be able to find the phrase with which my cruel and famous student, football hero Destructo Delbert Odell, has been taunting me. It isn't listed under "shake," and I cannot even find "thang."

I close my eyes and rest my forehead on page *Terrific–Thankful.* I can see Destructo tipped against the wall, balancing on the back legs of his chair, his muscular, clove-colored arms folded across his chest, his white slice of a grin. "Shake your groove thang, mama! Valeria, mama, shake that thang!"

The first day I was to teach Russian for Jocks (really called Russian with an Emphasis in Sports Vocabulary), I had asked the other teaching assistants why the department offered this special course for athletes. We were all four sitting in our office, having an early lunch of cheap caviar, Tab, and Marlboros. Do athletes have a special class, I asked, because they are part of the elite, like sons and daughters of wealthy businessmen?

"The elite," scoffed Marina, the best educated of us all, choking on laughter and cigarette smoke. "Bella says she had one boy who thought the Kremlin was a kind of cake. No, Russian for Jocks is just a way of having a Russian class for students who don't want to study. They get good grades, we get the enrollment."

As I walked to my classroom, through fog as dense as any I had ever seen huddling over a Russian potato field, I was frantic: what to say between

"Hello, I am your teacher, Valeria Chalisian" and "Now we will begin with the Cyrillic alphabet"?

Bella, who has great confidence and advice on everything, had advised: "They love to joke and clown around, those jock boys. Just be entertainment, Cookie." I kept seeing a semester of magic tricks and tap dances performed in front of the chalkboard, young giants in uniforms cheering me on.

The milky shapes of students on bicycles spun past me, their English cleck-cleck-clecking like the sound of playing cards clothespinned to the spokes. I lost the classroom twice. I wondered again why no American hospital would hire me as a nurse, because I didn't speak English, but a university would hire me as a teacher.

At the podium in front of the room, I removed my shawl slowly, buying time while I tried to gather up all the bits of English in my brain. The shawl is Armenian, a lovely black, bright with pink and turquoise flowers, which my mother-in-law gave me off her own shoulders at the airport before my husband and I disappeared into the West.

The jocks waited, quiet with curiosity. I got an inspiration and smiled. I remembered the fog that had detained me. The fog that had seemed so familiar.

"Hello. I Valeria Chalisian. I very sorry to be late." I nodded my head toward the window, and the gray-yellow clouds outside. I tried to hunt up the word lost. Instead I settled for: "Today there is much fuck."

I knew who Destructo Delbert Odell was already, because his picture was always on the front page of the sports section and because he often came to the Slavic Department to visit Pencil Neck, our student office worker. Destructo jutted out his lower lip, full and pink as a lung where it sloped inside his mouth. "What you say, mama?" He winked at another football player, sitting next to him.

"About fuck," I whispered. It sounded right in my head. I already felt I was losing blood. "Outside."

The only girl in the class chirped with laughter. She was wearing a sweatshirt that said MISSOULA, MONTANA. A PLACE. SORT OF. I stared hard at that sweatshirt, my cheeks thumping red, the laughter spreading around the room, contagious as measles. I knew what every one of those words meant. I knew them all, but they made no sense. It wasn't fair.

Today I am giving a quiz, and Destructo is not in class. As a matter of fact, none of the football team jocks are here. Only two fraternity brothers, who profess to have an interest in Russian sports vocabulary because they play intramural volleyball, are in attendance, also my Missoula, Montana girl. She explains that nobody came to class because we trounced Cal.

"But why winning game make him not to come?" I stammer.

"They're recuperating," the fraternity brothers say.

I am relieved to dismiss my class of three, even though I had planned to give a quiz and it makes me feel like a bad teacher to cancel. When I gave my last quiz, Destructo yowled and said, "What you tryin' to do to me, mama?" He spent the next forty-five minutes chewing on the cap of his pen until it was crunched into a wet blue pellet. On his paper, across the unanswered questions, he had written, "THIS SUX."

I went home and asked my husband what "THIS SUX" meant, and he murmured, "Oh, Valerinka, let me show you." He did, but I still do not understand why Destructo wrote it on his paper.

On afternoons I do not have to teach a class or attend one, I walk to the Russian store near our apartment. It is a long, thin space held captive between a fingernail salon and a dry cleaners. The dry cleaners is owned by the son of the proprietress of the store. In exchange for jars of Beluga caviar and California lottery tickets, he gives his mother the white cardboards around which pressed shirts are folded. She makes signs on these cardboards, tapes them to the tops of chopsticks, and thrusts them into the tired-looking meats and cheeses in her deli case. On bad days, seeing "Pastrami," "Tilsit," and "American Cheddar" rendered in her shaky Cyrillic has the same effect on me as hugging my grandmother's skirts.

My husband says the son is a true capitalist, forcing his mother to trade jars of Beluga for worthless paper. He says I feel the way I do about the signs not because I am homesick but because I have PMS.

It is a hot, smoggy day. The door of the store is held open by a cat sitting on a chair. Magna is rearranging a stack of dusty boxes of Kleenex.

"*Zdrastvuyte*, Magna Fyodorovna," I greet her.

She eyes me as if I am trying to sell her something, and wipes her dirty hands on her skirt.

There is nothing here I need. I pick up one of the boxes of Kleenex and one of two packages of Oreos, their labels bleached white from the sun. Magna is behind the cash register, looking through a mail order catalogue. She scratches her scalp with the end of her pencil. In the deli case I see a small cube of chocolate halvah, barely big enough to support its sign. I buy the halvah and ask Magna for the sign as well. She insists on wrapping it up special, apart from my other purchases.

While I am waiting for her to finish, I stare out the door. Cars flash past, chrome and color winking in the sun. As quickly as the cars, a man appears and disappears, carried past on long, lurching strides. It is Destructo. I hold my breath. What is he doing here?

I think at first he has run out of gas or missed his bus stop, but as I walk by the restaurant on the corner, one which my husband has identified as a greasy spoon, I see him sitting in a booth. He does not see me. There are several round metal tables outside, and without stopping to remember Grandmother's advice, that the price of curiosity is trouble, I sit down. I pull my shawl tighter around my shoulders and slide my packages onto the sticky circles left by a soda-pop bottle.

A man wearing a flannel shirt with no buttons is sitting across from Destructo. His black hair is decorated with slivers of broken leaves. He is reading from a newspaper as if he were a radio announcer. I hear words float out, words my jocks use: rush, monster, Heisman Trophy. When the waitress comes to take their order, Delbert speaks for the first time. "Order whatever you want," he says. The man drops the paper and rubs his hands together, his cuffs flopping around wrists spattered with flea bites.

At night, my husband, Catherine the Great, and I watch television; another project to help with the English. Tonight we are watching a program starring three men and their automobiles. My attention is divided between their adventures and the mysterious image of Destructo and the reading man.

"I love violence." My husband grins, scratching Catherine the Great behind the ear. On television, one of the villains has just been run over by a moving van.

"Violets?"

"Vio*lence.*"

"That is what I said," I lie in Russian. "Listen, you won't believe who I saw today up at the restaurant on the corner: Destructo Delbert Odell—you know, the big football star from my class."

"In English, Valeria, please," he says, not taking his eyes from the television.

"I can't explain it in English." I wasn't sure I could explain it at all.

"Valerinka, you must learn to go with the flow. That is the only way you will learn English."

"This is not a question of going with the flow," I retort. "It is a question of communicating. It is a very difficult thing to explain. There are things about it I cannot explain in English."

"You cannot explain about somebody sitting in a restaurant?"

"Never mind. I will ask someone at work."

My husband sighs. "All right. I'm listening."

"I said never mind." I stand up. "Don't do me any favors," I suddenly add in English. This phrase has occurred to me with great surprise and force; I simply didn't know I knew it. I feel the way I did when I stepped on an upturned garden rake hidden in the long grass on Grandmother's farm.

Next morning I am up early, doing everything double time to the rhythm of the English I'm talking in my head. "Don't do me any favors" has filled me with new confidence. I break up a Gaines•burger for

Catherine the Great; I poach an egg and burn some dark Russian rye for my husband. I am rehearsing what I will say to Pencil Neck. He will know about Destructo and the reading man. He takes coffee with Destructo several times a week and memorizes information about the football team. Pinning up my hair, I glance down at my English phrasebook. Pulling on my navy-blue tights, I murmur a phrase aloud: "I saw Destructo Delbert Odell in Russian neighborhood yesterday." It is not my voice. It is an American woman on television speaking English—low, breathy, and flat—but it is the only voice I know how to make English in. I drink Pepto-Bismol straight from the bottle, wandering around the apartment searching for my shoes.

I made up a quiz for today just so Pencil Neck and I would have a reason to converse. He is the only one in the department besides Claire, the secretary, who knows how to operate the mimeo.

When I arrive, Pencil Neck is sitting on the edge of Claire's desk, playing drums on his blue-jeaned legs with a ruler and a marking pen.

I hand him the Ditto master for the quiz, and I say to myself: "I am going to begin talking *now*." I also say it when he drops a ream of paper into the tray attached to the machine. And when he pours in the copying fluid.

The machine is loud: *chooka chooka chooka*, it says, providing me with an excuse to say nothing. Pencil Neck nods his head to the beat of the copying, his beige hair hopping off his forehead with each *chooka*. When the machine stops, he picks up the quizzes and lays them on his face, inhaling deeply. "Take a hit. It reminds me of second grade."

"I see Destructo," I blurt out. I know if I don't say something soon, opportunity will be lost.

"It couldn't have been in class." Pencil Neck's face opens into a chipped-tooth smile. It is okay. He is making a joke.

"No—at restaurant—at a restaurant—nearby to my house—in Russian neighborhood—far from university—from the university—a poor man reads to him. I ask me why? I ask me—"

"Probably because Del can't read," he says matter-of-factly.

"Del can't read," I repeat. This must be wrong. Everyone in America can read. I make a note to check the Gluzinsky.

"Of course not. Half the football team couldn't read the label on a bottle of beer if their lives depended on it."

I want to ask, "If Del can't read, then why is he so clever?" but all at once Pencil Neck bounces past me, springs into the air, fires one thin arm straight up, and drops an invisible ball into an invisible hoop. "Let's ask the man himself."

Destructo Delbert Odell has suddenly appeared in the doorway.

"Talk to me, talk to me," says Destructo to Pencil Neck, crooking his thumbs into his belt loops.

"Valeria here says she saw you having social intercourse with some major-league riffraff on Santa Monica Boulevard."

Slowly Destructo lifts his arms up and finds the top of the doorframe with his fingertips. "Oh, yeah?" His face snaps into his white grin, as if someone is about to take his photograph.

"Whatchoo doin' hangin' out in Russkiland, man?" Pencil Neck continues.

"I'm getting a little private-like tutoring on the side, huh, mama." He points his grin at me, but his eyes are startled, and cold as pebbles in a stream.

*  *  *

"There must be a reasonable explanation," I say to Vera Omulchenko, the department chairman. She has just handed me a computer printout sheet from the Registrar's Office. She says it is my final class list.

"I thought you had Delbert Odell in your class," she says. Her voice is soft and accusing. Rumor says she is a tough cookie. She is first-generation American, the daughter of well-educated Muscovites who were always on the right side of whatever regime was in power. She clicks one of her long, soft fingernails against her bottom teeth, waiting for my answer.

"He is in my class. I do not know why the name is not here." But to be honest, I should say that Delbert must have dropped my class. He wasn't there on Friday (I attributed it to preparing for The Game), on Monday (recuperating from The Game), or on Tuesday morning, when all the other football players tumbled in, grinning with new triumphs and fresh bruises.

Vera Omulchenko sighs. "You know you need to have seven students for the class to go."

"Yes, seven, I know."

She runs her hand up the back of her neck through her heavy blond hair. "Valeria, it does not look good for the department—having to drop classes because of low enrollment. I think you should contact Delbert and persuade him to rejoin your class."

I say of course I will, immediately. Instead I go home and try to read last week's Sunday sports section, which had a big story about Delbert. He is pictured in his uniform, clasping his helmet under one arm and the coach under the other. I sit at the kitchen table with my Gluzinsky, Catherine the Great asleep on my foot. I translate sentences about yardage gained, interceptions, and even Delbert's eleven brothers and sisters, who live in a place called Watts. I write all the important definitions in between the lines, but the lines are so close together that when I go back to reread it I cannot decipher anything. I rub my eyes, forgetting I have eye shadow on. I feel guilty, I deserve fruitless labor; I was reading only to discover if, hopefully, Delbert had been injured in last week's game, and that explained his absence from class.

Every afternoon for the next three days, I sit outside the greasy spoon, waiting for Delbert. I stay until the red lights of the nail salon blink on, but he and the reading man never appear. When I finally get up my courage to call, I discover that there is no telephone number for Destructo Delbert Odell.

The night before I track him down, I dream about him. It is brief and unnerving. I dream that we are lying together naked, but not yet as lovers. I am astonished at his body, so brown and massive, a piece of mountain between moon-white sheets. I am lying naked on his chest, my chin resting on the tops of my hands. We are not aware we are naked. "It's easier to be with you like this than to dance with you," I tell him. He lifts himself up on one elbow and stares at me. He is grateful to hear this, and I am aware of his gratitude. The passion leaps up like the blue-and-yellow flames of gas.

He lives in a place called the Mediterranean Apartments. Each letter in "Mediterranean" is a different tropical color.

When I knock on the door, he yells for me to come in. I think he is talking to someone already inside. In Soviet Union, people don't say "Come in."

Even if visitors are expected, doors are opened cautiously, only wide enough for a wedge of face. I knock again.

"It's open, man!" he calls. His voice is high and agreeable, expecting anyone else in the world but me.

I realize that I have never been inside a black person's apartment. There were no blacks in Kiev, although there was a slender, coppery-skinned woman from Ethiopia in my anatomy class. I cannot recall her face, but her English was perfect. She entertained us one day with a little ditty for remembering the cranial nerves: "On Old Olympus' Towering Tops a Finn and German Viewed Some Hops." It was the first complete English sentence I learned.

I go inside. There is a fuzzy shushing sound as the splintery bottom of the unfinished door passes over the green shag carpet. For an instant I panic: here I am entering Destructo Delbert Odell's apartment, trying to remember the cranial nerves, not paying attention.

He is in the small kitchen, peeling a carrot into a bowl of salad. The carrot and the peeler are bright and toylike in his giant fists. The Formica breakfast bar that divides living room from kitchen is set for two. Squares of yellow paper towel are wrapped around the silverware.

If I speak before he sees me, I can pretend it is my message he is unhappy about, not my presence. "Vera Omulchenko, department chairman, asks me to talk to you," I say primly.

"Well, hi, mama. You shoulda tol' me you was droppin' by. I make a mean borscht."

"I prefer to call, but you have not telephone."

He does not ask me in. I take a few steps toward the kitchen and find myself standing next to a tall, thin white metal box hanging on the wall. I study it, pretending interest. A sign on it says *Porn-O-Plenty Prophylactics*. Under the writing, a naked woman straddles an orange, which is rolling out of a huge curved horn. Other fruits are also rolling out. I peer closer.

"Those are watermelons?"

He hoots and points the peeler at the machine. "That is one fine cul-choo-ral artifact from the ladies' lounge at Notre Dame."

"Why are you not attending my class anymore?" I don't understand the Porn-O-Plenty, but I know it has nothing to do with why I am here.

"Sheeet, mama! You always spyin' on me."

"I do not spy. Just because I am Russian does not mean I spy."

"That so?" His smile flickers higher up his cheeks, which I notice for the first time are dotted with pinpoints of black freckles. His tone of voice is mocking and familiar. I am tired, my mouth sore from shaping English.

"Look. You were in greasy spoon nearby to my house on day I saw you. I walk by. I do not spy." My voice climbs higher with frustration. "I do not care if you cannot read."

He pulls another carrot from the cellophane bag on the counter, even though the salad is already hidden under a mound of orange shavings. "I can read," he says softly. He lies. I can tell.

"You did not need to stop coming to my class," I say. The only sound is the rhythmic skating of the peeler. "You know, I can't read English either. I can hardly speak it. And here I am, your teacher." The English pours out of my mouth. I am saying too much, talking because I suddenly can. The peeler clicks along faster and faster. "It is not your fault,"

I add, causing the hard black pebble look to spring into his eyes. He stabs the peeler into the air in front of my face.

"Listen, mama! You go tell Veera Omachenko and all those other fools that I's here to play football. I ain't here to rot in no classroom. All you sad sacks gonna be peddlin' Russian to boneheads while I'm makin' seven figures a year playin' for the Vikings."

Suddenly there is a spirited rap at the door, which shushes open over the carpet, admitting the reading man. He wears the same flannel shirt. He carries a rolled-up newspaper. "There you are, Del," he says in his loud broadcaster's voice. "Front page. 'Destructo Does It Again: Ducks Quack for Mercy.' "

I stare at the reading man as he shuffles over to his place at the breakfast bar.

"Pay no attention to that man behind the curtain," he says.

"What?" My voice is quavering. What man? What curtain?

"*The Wizard of Oz,*" he says. "I'm the Wizard."

"She's my Russian teacher," Delbert explains meekly.

"Russian," says the man. "How in the Lord's name you managing Russian, when you can't even get English?"

I hurry from Delbert's apartment to the bus stop through the dark. It isn't cold, but I pull my shawl closer out of habit. I have blown it, I think. I will never see Delbert again. My class will be canceled. My husband will be angry. I have blown it.

Abruptly, I stop. "I have blown it," I puzzle aloud, tasting the words, shocked to hear them. Two girls stepping out of a nearby car exchange amused glances over the roof. I try to trace the thought in my head. It did not travel the usual path from idea to Russian to English. There was, in fact, no Russian equivalent for it. "I have blown it," I say again, this time to the girls, who are shouldering book bags and purses and heading toward the university. I am disconcerted. I feel there is someone talking to me, but it is me talking to me. It is the brain of a bilingual person in action. It is me thinking in English.

As the girls stroll off to class, I notice they are wearing my favorite Top-Sider shoes.

"Hey, excuse me," I yell recklessly. "Where to buy those wonderful Top-Sider shoes?"

"Any department store," one of them calls back.

"Thank you," I cry.

I rush home to tell my husband.

# PRINCE MYSHKIN

## PENCIL NECK WEBER

At the Student Health Center, they won't let you see a real shrink unless you can prove you're straitjacket material or promise to pump a bullet through your head at the first opportunity. I wasn't onto this, though, and when I finally got up the courage to make an appointment, the apricot-haired receptionist sets me up with this thing called a student mental health advocate.

Student mental health advocates are recruited with fliers Xeroxed on cheap, bright paper, stapled to telephone poles around campus. The one I get is named Babe. She's a sorority type, a gold chain around her neck with a diamond *B* on it, and circles instead of dots over her *i*'s.

"I'm depressed, Babe," I tell her.

Somehow she looks familiar. She's real serious, and as she pulls her plump lips into a bunch, like a crinkled red flower, I recognize her as a student in Great Russian Books. This is a killer class taught by the Slavic Department, where I have a job for the semester, typing and filing for less than minimum wage.

"Has anyone died? Are you having trouble deciding on a career objective?" she asks.

"No, it's just . . . every day I walk around feeling like somebody's stuck an umbrella down my throat, then opened it. I'm like all flat inside."

Her lips bloom into a smile. So what else is new? People say I'm a riot when I'm miserable. They howl when I complain that a girl I've been seeing but don't really like has decided it's time we Date Other People, or that I can't get out of bed in the morning because the Red Sox lost the Series. And why shouldn't they? Most of my major bummers are the kind solved weekly on half-hour television programs. On the *first* half of half-hour television programs.

Once I tried to explain this to Serge, this Russian writer guy who teaches in the Slavic Department, at one of his parties. At 3 A.M., with only a few handfuls of potato chips standing between my stomach lining and a quart of Stolichnaya, I was nearly comatose under his coffee table, tears oozing out from the corners of my eyes, rolling into my hair. "It's not like I have any tragedies in my life," I said. "But there's nothing great about it either."

"No heaven, no hell," Serge said from somewhere in the depths of the apartment, "a blessing and a curse. Part of being an American."

"But hey! What can I do? I'm from Fresno. My father installs aluminum siding for a living."

Not a peep. He was racking his brain, or so I thought, for some profound Russian proverb. Then I heard him ease into bed, sigh, roll over. Into his pillow he muttered either "Pray to God" or "Try to jog." I've been trying to do both ever since, to cover my bases.

Babe's prescription is to keep a daily record of everything I have to be thankful for, a list of reasons for not being depressed. I force myself to go to the bookstore and shell out a buck for a notebook. When I get to the Slavic Department, I sit down and write:

*Reasons I Have For Not Being Depressed*

I chew on the inside of my mouth for a while, then add:

*1. I am not a Siamese Twin.*

A shuffle and a wheeze interrupt me. It's Professor Davidovich, crackling over the carpet on the static electricity generated by his ancient wing tips.

Like, I need this right now. He's always got a paper he wants me to type or a reason why I should change my major from Nothing to Russian. His papers are the worst. They have words in them like *podsudimykh* and *esteticheskie,* and I get brain-tumor headaches trying to force my fingers to stab the right combination of keys. Nobody cares about his work (how else are you supposed to feel about "The Role of the Dog in Mikhail Kuzmin's 'Aunt Sonia's Sofa' "?), and at this very moment his last masterpiece is doing the newspaper-at-the-bottom-of-the-birdcage routine in Vera's in box. Vera's the department chairman and normally *inhales* all this boring junk. Now, why isn't *he* depressed? He should be.

"Here are the examinations, Pencil," he says. He thinks my nickname, Pencil Neck (the insult, added by my brother, to the injury of being tall, skinny, and sort of yellow), is my real name. First name Pencil, last name Neck. He positions a file folder over my notebook. "You know, I dipped into a little Mayakovsky this weekend and thought of you. He's a wonderful poet, very accessible to young people. Of course, he did have a bit of a problem making the transition to the twentieth century, despite what he professed, but never mind, we can discuss this at my End of the Year Celebration. You can make it, can't you?"

"Sure. I'll try," I say. That'll be the day, I think. Davidovich puts this thing on every year, and only a few old Russians from around town, unemployed gin rummy players who've spent their lives in the park around the La Brea Tar Pits dealing cards under the pounding sun, and a couple of okay professors usually show up.

"Good, good! I'll bring the Mayakovsky. In any case, here are my examinations. All you must do is see that everyone gets one, then collect them at the end of the period." Davidovich is having periodontal surgery on the last day of his Advanced Russian Syntax class, and because no one else will do it, I've agreed to administer his final exam.

The entire graduate population of the Slavic Department is in this class: one American mom who's back in school getting her M.A. and the Lenin Sisters—four Russian ladies, not related, who at one time or another all tried to get jobs teaching Elementary Russian. They were told by Chairman Vera that they didn't have the proper credentials to teach. It's true, they don't. Then Vera, in a kind of creepy move, encouraged them instead to enroll in the Graduate Program. To everyone's satisfaction, they did. Now they are all graduate teaching assistants, teaching Elementary Russian. They get half the salary of a regular instructor.

They share a dinky office at the end of the hall. Most days I do my work to the accompaniment of high-pitched Russian swearing, slamming doors, and general top-of-the-lung arguments. They throw things at each other to decide who are the greatest living Russian writers. Once I had to break up a hair-pulling scuffle brought on by a discussion of Mrs. Gorbachev's wardrobe.

Worse, though, is when they make up. Giggles, tears, and vodka—even in the middle of a Tuesday morning. Now, I'm no prude, I've come drunk to work, stoned too, especially lately, but think how it is, pecking away at "Aleksandr Ablesimov: The Man Who Changed the Face of 18th Century Russian Comic Opera," while four grown women are forgiving one another, remembering Russian folk dances from their childhood, and performing them around the mimeograph machine.

They force you to join in, clutch at your elbows, yank you out of your seat, and do the thing you hate most. They call you Prince Myshkin. "Prince Myshkin! Come, you must be my partner! Prince Myshkin, watch me! Put your hand on my waist, there! Oh, look, we've embarrassed him now. Oh, poor Prince!" It's mortifying.

It was Tanya who started with this Prince Myshkin business, the night I took her and Valeria to see *The Brothers Karamazov*. It wasn't a date or anything, even though Tanya is the only one of them I could consider my type if I did a major stretch of my imagination. She has nice rippled sand-colored hair, like an old-fashioned damsel in distress, and skitters around the department in those three-inch-high heels called mules.

Stuck in my Mazda in six-o'clock traffic, watching the sun bloody the rooftops as it cut behind them, Tanya told me that when she was a kid she'd had a small part in *The Brothers Karamazov* but that her scenes had been chopped out.

"Even so," she said, "I could see that film a hundred times, each time wondering how different my life would have been if they had kept me in." She snuggled back into my sheepskin seat cover, getting cozy with this sorrowful thought. She had been a big actress in Leningrad, and now she spends all her free time and money paying a dialogue coach to get rid of her Russian accent, so that she can go about becoming a big actress here.

"You are not only person—the only person— with the life that is a has-been," said Valeria.

In the rearview mirror I could see her watching for a parking place, concentrating hard, like somebody bent on finding stars in the smoggy nighttime sky. Her black-and-gray hair was pulled straight back from her wide, bony face in a bun. Popping out of the bun was a long bobby pin, a lone antenna. Like an unzipped dress, an open fly, spinach snagged between front teeth. My eyes dropped back down and focused on the bumper ahead of me. Valeria's one of those you-gotta-give-her-credit-for-trying types, but it gets excruciating.

"There! 'Truck Loading Zone. No Parking Six A.M. to Eight P.M. Mon–Fri,' " she cried. I was halfway into the spot by the time she finished with the sign. I could feel her happiness and sense of accomplishment spilling over into the front seat, just because she was able to read the English.

Before the previews of coming attractions, the guy who sold us our popcorn and Junior Mints announced that they wouldn't be able to show *The Brothers Karamazov* because they had received two reel ones and no reel two. Tanya sighed: "It isn't as though I haven't seen it before."

Valeria said, "Maybe we will get cinema—*a* cinema?—*some* cinema? in English."

What we got was what the theater was going to show the next night, *Serpico*, with Al Pacino.

Like, I admit the movie is really '70s, but once you get past the bell bottoms it's great. Al Pacino is this cop, straight from cop school, with incredible ideals. But he's not a geek. He's got a motorcycle and a nickname, Paco. Long hair, because that was the hip thing then. His first day on the job, he goes into this dumpy little restaurant and orders a roast beef sandwich. His partner tells him he's supposed to take whatever the special is, because the restaurant owner gives them lunch every day for free as payment for looking the other way. But Pacino won't take it. He won't compromise himself even that much, on this smallest of issues. He says, "No way," and pays for the roast beef. Then he goes on to expose the corruption of the whole New York Police Department (everyone from the men's room attendant on up is taking bribes) and gets shot in the face. He doesn't die, but you get the feeling that he would have, he believed that much in what was right. This movie *slayed* me. I cried in the end, but I didn't let any tears come out.

Afterward, Bella and Marina met us at a restaurant across the street for cheap Mexican food. It's the worst place in town, but they insisted on it because you get beets on your tostada.

"We saw the silliest movie," said Tanya. "About a vain man who didn't have the good sense to take the money that was offered him."

I stared at her. She has a big curvy Minnie Mouse smile, which she trots out for all occasions, and she smiled over her margarita glass. This is just the kind of thing she normally comes out with, not realizing how ridiculous she sounds.

"I saw *Serpico* several years ago. In Paris," said Marina. The other teaching assistants don't like Marina because she went to the best college in Moscow and still hangs on to her Soviet passport. She's sophisticated. She has posters of Argentina and Istanbul over her desk and goes to topless bars with her American husband. She lit a colored cigarette and used the edge of her plate for an ashtray.

"I thought you were going to see *The Brothers K?*" said Bella. "Now I am glad I went to Glendale Galleria President's Day Sale instead. I got a very beautiful tote bag. This is similar tote bag to Cricket's. You know my friend Cricket. Salesgirl at Bullock's." She pulled the bag up from where it rested against her knees under the table. It was real cutesy, with a lavender cat in a bikini on it, relaxing in a chaise longue, and another cat throwing a beach ball. She stroked one of the cats' cheeks. "It's so lovely. Perfect for boating, picnicking, or just around town."

"I thought the movie was okay," I interrupted, before Bella got started on the subject of shopping. "I mean, I'm not an expert on movies or anything, but I thought it was okay."

"It was preposterous," said Tanya. "Who could believe such a story?"

"But it's *true*," I said. "Serpico lives in Switzerland now."

Tanya laughed. She reached over and tried to cover my hand with hers, but you'd need a catcher's mitt for that (I'm six feet five), so she settled for capturing my knuckles. "Truly, you are Prince Myshkin for a modern age."

The rest of them started in with the giggles, like this was the funniest thing going.

Great, I thought, who in the hell is Prince Myshkin? I went through my mental Rolodex of all the princes I knew: Prince Charles, Prince Andrew, Prince Rainier, the dead Freddie Prinze, the tennis racket Prince, the rock star Prince.

"Yes, I can see it—that," said Valeria. "When does you use 'it' and when does you use 'that'? Or is it do you—do you or does you?"

"Oooh, Cookie, yes! Yes!" Bella beat her palms together in applause, careful not to endanger pink dagger fingernails. "An American Prince Myshkin."

Marina narrowed her eyes, checking me out. "Yes," she said, "like your husband, Tanyichka."

I felt Tanya's hand grow moist. "You are not to make light of my husband."

"I am not making light. I am making a comparison. Like our Prince here, he is a bit unclear of things, is he not?"

Tanya's husband, locked away somewhere in the Soviet Union, is a big topic of conversation around the office and behind Tanya's back. The stories are all different, depending on which teaching assistant you talk to and whether she's just had a fight with Tanya.

Apparently, he is (or isn't) a Soviet dissident who circulated a petition to get the heat turned on in their apartment building because Tanya was (or lied to him that she was) pregnant. He was arrested for trying to start a riot (which he was or wasn't trying to do), either out of his own carelessness or because Tanya turned him in to the KGB in exchange for a passport to the United States, something she wanted because she's Jewish (or because her acting career or her relationship with her husband was going nowhere). I'm not sure I buy any of it. Who gets arrested for circulating a petition, even in Russia? What wife turns her husband in for trying to get heat in the apartment?

"You are a KGB provocateur," Tanya spat at Marina.

Bella, coming to Marina's defense, accused Tanya of having the heart of a capitalist and the soul of an informer. Valeria tried to confirm that there was a difference between "sole" and "soul." Tanya's hand leapt off mine and hurled a dish of salsa at Bella, who ran to the ladies' room, screeching "Adrienne Vittadini, my Adrienne Vittadini!" Now, who's *that*, I thought, another wigged-out Russian lady I'd have to deal with? But Marina pushed two streams of smoke through her perfect nostrils and told me that Bella was just squawking about her blouse.

While they do their exams, I sit at the front of the room and try to write in my journal. I keep getting confused. For example, I write that one of the reasons I have for not being depressed is that at least I know I have a job this summer when school gets out. Then, under *Reasons Why I Am Depressed* (a new heading I created when I ran out of reasons for not being depressed), I put down what the job was: picking figs back home in Fresno. I write down under reasons I shouldn't be depressed: my parents aren't divorced. Then write down under reasons I should be depressed: my parents aren't divorced. In the end, I figure out what I've always known, that I have no real reasons to be depressed or not to be depressed. If you could draw a picture of my life, it would look like the line on a heart monitor connected to a dead person: Graduation, Job, New Car, Love Affair Dwindling into Marriage, Baby, Raise, Baby, New Car, Younger Lover, Divorce, Even Younger Lover Who Leaves Me, Retirement. I lay my head down on the desk and close my eyes.

I lie like this for a minute, maybe minutes. Thoughts and images that don't normally go together link up and start forming the beginning of a dream, when I hear "Move your hand." It's Tanya's voice. I recognize the burr in it, from too much smoking and screaming. In the dark little cave of my arms, I like hearing it; I start getting into imagining it in a dark bedroom.

"I can't tell if it's a *g* or an *s*," she whispers. This punches me awake. My head snaps up. This is what I see: Tanya cheating off of Bella, who's cheating off of Marina, who's cheating off of Valeria, who's harvesting all the answers from skinny Doris Bell, the American mom. Doris hunkers her skinny shoulders down over her paper, trying to keep her answers to herself.

In a fraction of a second I get the picture. Boy, do I. My glance shoots down and sticks on an empty page in my journal. In that instant I've become what you never imagine yourself to be: the guy who hears screaming outside his apartment late at night and turns up the television set so he can pretend he doesn't notice it.

For two hours I sit that way, writing sometimes, but mostly just pretending like I'm concentrating, while the whispering, paper shuffling, and chair repositioning rage on around me.

That night, neither my roommate nor I have a date, so we eat some of his Cornish game hens with prosciutto. Besides being a physics major, my roommate cooks gourmet for a hobby. There's a plaque on his bedroom wall next to his Madonna poster that says he won first place somewhere for his white chocolate mousse.

There's nothing on the tube but some dumb speech by the President, and we both agree that we need a night off before we start cramming for finals. We decide to see a movie. He's seen everything I want to see and I've seen everything he wants to see and the only things we both haven't seen are things we don't want to see, so we end up at *Serpico* at the Criterion, playing on a double bill with *Stripes* as part of their Friday-night Men in Uniform series.

I try not to think of it, the cheating, and for a while I do okay. But then Pacino's black droopy eyes and pasty face, twenty feet tall, start working on me. The theater is very dark, no green EXIT signs hanging over the doors on either side of the screen, and with only my roommate slouched next to me, and not Tanya, with her soft, almost hairless arm fighting with mine for space on the worn armrest, I get lost. I'm reduced to two eyes watching and a brain perceiving, stuck on a pole made of flesh.

The next day, I get my ear pierced like Serpico. While I stand in line at the May Company, where they are having Free Ear-Piercing, Saturday Only, with three teenage girls who have sixteen holes in their collective ears, and a guy with a long, silky green Mohawk, I make an entry in my journal:

*Reasons Not To Be Depressed*
1. I'm going to tell Davidovich the truth.

My turn comes, and I'm too tall to sit in the chair, so the ear piercer, all nurselike in a fresh white pantsuit, makes me kneel on the floor. I make a joke out of it, putting my hands together in prayer, toss-

ing off a few one-liners about being knighted, Sir
Pencil Neck, Knight of the May Company Jewelry
Counter, but when she gets down to business and a
tight column of pain blasts through my earlobe, I
feel good and strong.

Monday morning, an angry pink halo of infec-
tion surrounds the post I had to buy to get the free
piercing.

I stride into the department to the beat of my
pulse banging in my ear. But the pain is okay; it reminds me of my purpose. The Lenin Sisters will
probably lose their jobs over this, I think. I suddenly
imagine them among the decrepit gin rummy players
at the Tar Pits, living on welfare and passing their
empty days reminiscing about Kiev or Moscow. I like
feeling bad about this.

I've lost track of Davidovich's party, and it turns
out to be today. Folding chairs are set up around the
office, and the secretary's desk has been cleared off
to make way for the goodies. Davidovich is stooped
down in the corner, plugging in a record player. I
start to lose my nerve. "Pencil, you're here! *Khorosho.*" He stands hastily. "Come help me with the
borscht."

I follow him back to his office. On his desk is a
platter of cold cuts; a tub of potato salad sits where
the wastebasket used to be. On the file cabinet, an
electric pot simmering with borscht fills the air with
a dark, sour smell.

"And this, this," he says. "My wife made it."
From behind his desk he lifts a plate with a tall,
skinny tin pyramid balanced on it, the point as sharp
as a spear.

"What is it?"

"Paska," he whispers. "Pure and pearly white.

It's traditionally an Easter dessert, but it's a dessert of liberation as well, and that's why I serve it at the end of the year." He takes the pyramid by the palms of his shaky hands and gently, reverently, lifts it up. Under it is an identical pyramid of white cheese, dotted with raisins. "This mold is an antique from the Ukraine," he says. "My wife inherited it from her mother, who, as the family story goes, dragged it across Russia with her when she was fleeing the Red Army."

"Cool," I say. "Listen, we gotta talk." I hear people in the front office; I want to get this over with. "I think—well, you're not gonna like this. On that exam I gave to the Russian syntax class—well, they—I think they cheated a little."

"Yes, I know."

"You *know?* Did Doris Bell tell you?" Now I feel cheated.

"All of their mistakes were the same." He runs his forefinger around the base of his paska, then licks it.

"Well, aren't you supposed to like flunk them or fire them or something?"

When a herd stampedes, you hear it before you see it. I know this from westerns on television.

Suddenly there is the *clop clop* of heels on linoleum, the *swipe swipe* of legs in panty hose rubbing against each other. Tanya, her face hot, fists clenched, marches into the room, followed by the others. "You want him to fire us? Why is that? Answer me that!"

"I should have mentioned how the sound carries," says Davidovich.

"I didn't say that."

"We heard you." Bella pushes her way past Tanya. She has done something to her hair, had it whipped and dipped for the party, I guess, and it makes her look even angrier than she is. "You told to him that we cheated on our exams."

"You did cheat on your exam," I say. I nervously twirl the post in my ear. Serpico is shaking his head. Even he'd back off from this one.

"We were only to try to pass examination," says Valeria, more sensible than the rest. "Mr. Davidovich has tells us that we must succeed to pass it."

"But honestly—we do things *honestly* in America."

"What about Allende's Chile," asks Marina coldly. All I can think about is my roommate's chili, a special recipe using beer and sugar.

"You accuse us of being dishonest?" Tanya gets closer.

"No one said you were dishonest," says Davidovich.

"You're not supposed to cheat on your exams," I say. "In this country we do not cheat on our exams. Look, you wouldn't let your students cheat, would you?"

"No, but they are the students and we are the teachers!"

"But in this class *you're* the students."

"We is teachers," says Valeria, tight-lipped and self-righteous. "As teachers we have privileges."

"But one of them is not cheating on your final," I say desperately.

"It is an insult that we even have to take a final," says Marina.

This is crazy. I look to Davidovich for reinforcement, but he's engrossed in arranging some wilted lettuce on a plate. Finally, he looks up and says, "Nobody is ever interested in lettuce at these kinds of functions, but one must make an attempt. I can't get rid of them, Pencil. Native Russian speakers who would teach for so little money are impossible to find."

"All right," I say, "forget it."

"I won't forget it," says Tanya, grabbing my wrist. Her stubby fingertips press in so hard I feel like my tendons are going to split apart.

"Oh, Cookie, leave him alone. Prince Myshkin is a good boy," says Bella, pumping up her dimples. "Prince Myshkin, we will make sure that in future times we do not cheat while you are watching, okey-doke?" She coyly rests her chin on Tanya's shoulder. This is a mistake.

"I won't forget it." Tanya pulls my face down to hers. "I don't forget informers."

I stare down into her pupils, and for that one moment, that tiny blip in time, my strength is equal to hers; I'm no frail pencil neck, immobilized by an uneventful life.

"That makes two of us," I whisper, soft as a confession of love.

"*I am not an informer!*" Her hand curls into a fist, but as she pulls it back, aiming to throttle me, she violently shrugs Bella off her shoulder. I can hear Bella's jaws smash together, a tiny bud of tongue caught between her teeth. Bella howls. She teeters back on her heels, cupping her jaw in her hand. But she's like a pendulum, and as she swings forward she thrusts out her arms and gives Tanya the shove of her life, sending her skidding out of her mules and across the platter of cold cuts on Davidovich's desk. And with the stubbornness that got Tanya out of the Soviet Union, with the determination that turns people into actresses and dictators, she refuses to release my wrist. She hauls me along with her. I stumble into the tub of potato salad. I flatten the paska with my fist. I break my fall with the antique pyramid mold from the Ukraine.

I put all this down in my journal, while I wait at the Health Center to get two stitches at the place where the point of the pyramid ripped through my shorts and drew blood. The physician's assistant who takes my temperature tries not to laugh when I tell her the story behind the wound, but while I'm lying pantless on my stomach, waiting for the doctor to show up, I hear her retelling it on the telephone to one of her friends.

Two days later, I have my next appointment with Babe. She asks to read my journal. She wonders, flipping through it, if I've utilized it in the proper manner. She uses that word, "utilized." She sees the new headings, the days I neglected to write, my harangue about the Russians, my account of how I nearly got lead poisoning doing something I thought might be right. The harangue interests her, though, and she lays the notebook down flat, parking her cheekbones on her palms, bending forward to read.

"Hm," she says. "What did you learn from all this?"

"It's good Serpico didn't die."

"Who?"

"A friend of mine."

"Uh-huh," she says. She stands up suddenly, shyly, looking down at her fingers, spread on her pink cotton skirt. "I'll be back in a second, all right?"

She hurries out of the white cubicle, leaving me alone with a wall chart on how to perform CPR. I read the chart, and when she still doesn't come back, I pick up a book lying next to her notebook. I recognize it as one taught in the Great Russian Books class, something called *The Idiot.* Inside the book are several sheets of notebook paper. I unfold them, hoping it might be a letter, something juicy. It's a term paper. The first sentence goes: "The Idiot, Prince Myshkin, is one of Dostoevsky's most appealing and long-suffering heroes."

At that moment she returns, flushed and relieved. "I just talked to Dr. Schaeffer; he's the psychologist, who comes in once a week. He said he could see you right now, if you want."

As I follow her down the hall, watching her hips make her skirt move, I suddenly don't feel so depressed.

# TRESPASSERS WELCOME HERE

## SERGEI LUBLINSKY

My son, Boris, gives me an ascot for Christmas every year. In honor of him, and this day, I decide on the orange paisley, the last one I received before emigrating to the United States, an East German import for which he traded his only record album, a bootleg copy of *The Kinks' Greatest Hits*.

Have you ever heard of Velcro? I have a thin blue strip of it traversing the back of my closet. This is where the ascots hang, like a cache of international flags.

Coming outside my apartment, I run into Pencil Neck, my next-door neighbor and manager of the apartment complex. He is leaning out over the swimming pool with a net on the end of an aluminum pole, catching empty beer cans and wine bottles.

"It appears you have another blowout-style party last night," I say.

"Yeah. I spent the whole night riding the porcelain bus." He stabs me with a sly look, which, due to his great height, comes from the bottoms of his gray eyes instead of the corners. He is trying to catch me with another colloquialism. But I am a tough customer, nobody's fool, and was not born yesterday.

"I know. I heard you," I say. "Los Angeles and Moscow have this in common—thin walls."

"Is there any lingo you *don't* know?" He half-heartedly pursues a bottle of Chablis around the shallow end.

"Of course! 'What's the haps?' confused me last week only."

"It means like 'What's happening?' "

"Ah. I see. Then here is a haps for you. I'm having a party myself, to celebrate my official emigration. Come tomorrow evening around eight. And feel free to bring—what is her name—Amy?"

"One of the many that got away."

"Already she left you?"

"How can somebody leave you when they weren't with you in the first place?" He captures the bottle and hurls the net over his shoulder. I expect to hear glass shattering, but hear nothing instead. He drops the net back in the pool, only the bottle is still there, entangled in the webbing.

I clap him on the shoulder. "Well, you can bring yourself, and perhaps some munchies for eating."

Claire Davis is the secretary at the university's Department of Slavic Languages and Literatures, where I hold the curious position of writer in residence. I was offered this position by Vera Omulchenko, department chairman and old friend, before I was officially asked to leave Moscow. For months I had visions of sleeping on a cot in my office, like a doctor working nights in an emergency ward: Sergei Lublinsky, writer in residence, on call twenty-four hours a day to answer your most urgent and intimate questions on contemporary Russian literature and emigration.

Claire has agreed to guide me to the Immigration Office this special day, and when I arrive at the department she is inhaling a health-food bar and talking to one of the teaching assistants, Marina.

"*Dobrya utra*, Sergei Pavlovich," Marina yawns.

"*Dobrya utra*, Marina." I do my best to be civil.

She reluctantly looks at me. With one brown eye and one green eye, her insolent gaze, invented and perfected by Russian women born into the privileged class, is even more infuriating. I have heard from the grapevine that she does not like my work. Even though six of my novels have been published in as many languages, and I sacrificed my Soviet citizenship for *Trespassers Welcome Here*, she feels I do not deserve my position here. "See you later, Claire," she says. She wanders off toward her office. My shoulders relax.

"How are tricks with you today, Claire Davis?"

"Listen: *Ya liublu kliukvu!*"

"You like cranberries?"

She tosses the wrapper from the health-food bar into the wastepaper basket beside her desk and picks up her shoulder bag. "It's to practice the 'yew' sound. Marina taught it to me. So do you have your new car?"

Miraculously, I do. It arrived yesterday, just in time for me to pick up my papers in style. Have you heard of the color oyster? This is the color of my new car, an Oldsmobile Cutlass. The upholstery is periwinkle-blue crushed velvet. I waited for a car with this special interior for nearly as long as I waited for my first typewriter in Moscow.

The car is parked at the back of the parking lot, angled over two spaces the way I saw a Mercedes-Benz parked at the supermarket.

"Sergei, it's dynamite!" cries Claire, clearly going hog wild.

"I am forty-four years old, and this is the first object I have ever owned that costs more than three hundred dollars."

"I bet you tell that to all the girls."

"I do not pull your leg about something like this, Claire Davis."

As I open the passenger door for her, I notice a very short, very wide Sergei Lublinsky reflected in the car door. I am not surprised to see myself, a rather attractive middle-aged Russian man in a jogging suit, helping a brash American girl into a new Oldsmobile Cutlass, but I am surprised to see how natural it looks. Only my teeth, colored brown from black Russian tea, strong tobacco, and little dental care, give a clue as to my nationality. But I can smile very nicely with my lips closed (see my picture on the back of *Don't Say Russian When You Mean Soviet*), and I do so now.

"So you like it, do you?"

"I had a VW once, named Poubelle. That's French for garbage can. Then that car got totaled, and now the car I have is even worse, and it's called Poubelle Two: The Final Chapter. After this I'm getting a Porsche." Claire Davis answers all my questions with such anecdotes, which I'm sure she invents just to be amusing. She is like my son, Boris, that way.

*   *   *

The day before I left Moscow, Boris and I were having tea at the restaurant on the corner by his school. He had been studying architecture at Moscow State University, but two hours after I had my birth certificate and passport confiscated, he was booted from the university, erased from the rolls of the Young Communist League—to his secret relief— and redirected to a technological institute for refrigerator and air-conditioning parts manufacturers.

It was our last meal together, but we acted as though I were just going on vacation or to a writers' conference. We slurped and blew on our *shchi* (cabbage soup) and talked about another time we had eaten here and I had found a Band-Aid in my soup, folded over in thirds, straight from someone's finger. I didn't have my glasses on and had thought perhaps it was a mushroom. Boris laughed so hard remembering this that he swallowed wrong. I gave him a few thumps on the back, realizing, for the first time, that my square peasant's hand barely fit between my son's bony, narrow shoulder blades.

"You must eat more, gain some weight."

"So I can look like those fat old guys in bikinis at the Black Sea? No, thank you."

So you can last, I wanted to say.

I notice that in California only older people drive the way they tell you to in the Driver's Training Manual, so I keep both hands together at the bottom of the steering wheel and hope I can maintain control of such a big piece of machinery. Although it is only February, it must be nearly eighty degrees outside, and I roll down my window and put my arm out, feeling the breeze blow against my palm. How can doing something so simple make one feel so young? I reach over and pop my favorite Dizzy Gillespie tape into the cassette machine that is built into the dashboard. I cannot tell if Claire likes the music or not.

She is looking down at a thin book in her lap, one she has brought along, I foolishly suppose, to occupy her while I am conducting my business. Claire Davis is a tall girl, so tall that her head is only inches from the roof of the car, which is also upholstered in the periwinkle blue. Something electrical is going on between her curly red-brown hair and the upholstery, because every time she turns her head even slightly, one or two more hairs drift up from the top of her head and affix themselves to the roof.

"You are sticking to the ceiling. It must be the magnetic personality." I pass my hand over her head. The hairs spring up again anyway.

"What?" I've surprised her. I withdraw my hand, and it is at that moment I see what she is reading: *Point of Pride* by Gennady Blizitsky.

"What . . . where did you get that?" I have never seen that collection of lies and insinuations in an English edition. The cover is shiny black, with a red hammer and sickle perched behind an old-fashioned American typewriter. On the back of this waste of a publisher's time and materials is undoubtedly *his* photograph.

"Serge! Jesus Christ!"

I look up through the windshield. The Oldsmobile is straying toward an unsuspecting herd of shoppers tearing through racks of clothing at a sidewalk sale. Luckily, however, my eyes are somehow in cahoots with my feet, and during these past two or three horrifying moments the car hasn't been getting any gasoline. We roll into the curb and stop. The shoppers throw us a collective irritated glance and

go back to their bargains. Someone passing on a motorcycle informs me I'm an asshole.

"May I see that?" I ask Claire. My voice has not
shaken like this since I asked that Soviet bag of slime
who arranged for my United States visa why Boris
would not be allowed to emigrate with me.

"What's the big deal?"

"Just give to me! Please." I am ready to pull her
arms off. She senses this and hands it over.

As I suspected, on the back cover of this Party-
appeasing impersonation of a work of art is Gennady
Blizitsky, also sitting behind a typewriter. He is
wearing a silk shirt (you must have many silk shirts,
Gennady Ilyich, now that you are the darling of the
Bosses) and coyly chews on the end of the earpiece
of his wire-rim glasses.

"How is it you read this piece of crap?" I shout.

"I'm interested, that's all."

"Only an idiot could find anything remotely interesting in such rubbish."

"Tell that to Marina. She's teaching it in her
class. She happens to find it intriguing."

"Intriguing! Intriguing!"

Claire wets her finger and rubs at a scratch on
the face of her watch.

"He . . . he is a hack, Claire Davis. A hack!"

She slowly turns her head and looks at me. "He
probably says the same thing about you."

Since I left the apartment complex this morning, someone has thrown a lounge chair in the pool.
The frame must harbor some hidden air pockets, because the chair hovers inches above the drain, as
though by magic. Every time I swim over it I ache to
dive down and sit in it, forcing the chair to the bot-

tom and drowning myself in the process. I have picked up my damned papers, chauffeured the duplicitous Claire Davis back to the Slavic Department, and flung myself into the pool, where I am swimming my daily mile.

Due to the nice weather, clusters of students are lounging around. They wag their feet to the beat of the rock music issuing from Pencil Neck's stereo and allegedly study. Sometimes they call to me: "Hey, Serge, only 3,830 laps to go!" "Hey, Serge, doesn't that make you dizzy?" "Hey, Serge, whadda they call that, Russki Dog Paddle?" I usually enjoy their teasing, but today I am thankful for my nose plug, ear plugs, and goggles: it is the next best thing to being nowhere.

I imagine the scenario at the department as I puff up and down the pool. Claire Davis screeches with enthusiasm, telling that venomous Marina the story of the greasy tire mark that now scars Gennady Blizitsky's chin on Marina's personally autographed copy of *Point of Pride*. "Oh, Marina, that Sergei Pavlovich is a real Russian crackpot. After he called Gennady Blizitsky a hack, he threw the book out the window, right into the middle of the street."

And what would Marina say to that? "You must understand, Claire Davis, that Sergei has a reputation for flying off handles, stepping out of line, and rocking boats. Why do you think he was forced to leave Soviet Union? Why do you think his son, his intelligent black-haired boy, is doomed to make a living producing air conditioners? Why do you think, even now, the KGB has an open file on him?"

And now they are laughing, Marina with her face toward the ceiling so her audience can appreciate the best view of her fine Russian nose. It was she who suggested to Claire Davis that reprehensible

crock of Politburo-loving crap. (Flabby-minded Claire
Davis, who gives the same attention to biographies
of wrinkled Hollywood actresses that she gives to
*War and Peace.)*

"And if you are really interested in a good laugh,
just let Sergei Pavlovich see you reading it," Marina
may have said. Or maybe she was more forceful than
that: "Claire Davis, take this book in the car with you
and report back to me all that Sergei Pavlovich says."
After all, wouldn't Marina love to see me make a
horse's ass out of myself? Gennady Blizitsky is a
friend of hers (how else would she have in her possession the autographed copy?), and even though he
now has closets full of fine silk shirts and a cozy
country dacha outside Moscow, it is my work that is
reviewed by the *New York Times* and included in
anthologies.

Perhaps Marina and Gennady exchange letters
about me even now, or maybe, on her next visit to
Moscow, they will dine together at the Writers Union.
"Sergei Pavlovich is still screaming and raving about
you, Gennady Ilyich," she'll say. "He is still calling
you a hack. He imagines himself an American, but
he's still a Russian screwball, hurling books out the
window in the middle of downtown Los Angeles and
threatening the life of our department secretary just
because she's reading your book."

It is ironic that they both attended Moscow
State, I think to myself on lap number 107. It is the
only school in the entire Soviet Union where you
could empty every classroom asking for volunteers
to inform for the KG—

I choke on a mouthful of water laced with chlo-
rine and beer. I cough and struggle to the side of the
pool. I hear Pencil Neck—I think it's Pencil Neck; I'm
blind without my glasses—say, "Hey, man, are you

all right?" But now I know what I've always suspected: Marina is KGB.

There are KGB all over the world, not full-fledged agents but informers, collaborators, and friends. Of course there is one, at least one, monitoring the activities of the Slavic Department of a large American university. And isn't it interesting that she arrived on the scene only one week before I did?

I lie in bed, not even trying to sleep. Everything fits. The reason they would not allow Boris to emigrate was not to punish me but to protect themselves. There was no effective way to silence me in Moscow without raising the suspicion and sympathy of Western journalists and governments, so they allowed me to leave. And now my son is like the shapely girl in an old American gangster flick, whose head will get blown off if I make one false move. It occurs to me that I haven't received a letter from him in nearly four months, and I wonder if this means anything. Certainly my opinion of Gennady Blizitsky hasn't reached them already?

Suddenly there is a sound. I'm drifting into a dream starring Humphrey Bogart, Boris, and a girl I was in love with one winter, who would skate alone every day in Gorky Park. I think the noise is part of the dream, and I ignore it. Then it comes again: the crunching of gravel. Someone is walking with great care just beneath my window. I sit up and stare into the darkness. I put on my glasses, and the darkness comes into focus.

An old friendly thought comes to mind: They never come after 11:00. I used to tell this to Boris. It was a bold-faced lie, of course. They came anytime they felt the urge. When he was three, his mother, my wife, was confiscated just past midnight, along with everything I had ever written. But I told my son, my big boy of nearly twenty years, terrified of going to sleep for fear of being jolted awake by over-coated officers, that those bad old days were gone, that now they had rules and restrictions, and they were forbidden to break in between the hours of 11:00 P.M. and 5:00 A.M.

Outside, the person passes my window. Then I hear, in a loud, wobbly whisper: "Hey, creep face, it's me. Open the door. You put the stupid chain on the door, man." It's only Pencil Neck, talking at the bedroom window of his roommate.

"I thought you were at Kathy's tonight," says the roommate. He is a student in physics, and I know him only as the oaf, which is what Pencil Neck calls him behind his back.

"So did I," mumbles Pencil Neck. "Now would ya just open up?"

Will I confront her? Or will we do the dance of the dissident and his shadow? I wonder as I drink from a bottle of Stolichnaya, so chilly the tips of my fingers stick to it briefly before I set it down.

Across the room, Marina is holding court on the sofa. Claire Davis sits cross-legged at her feet (even Gennady Blizitsky could not dream up so obvious a metaphor), and next to her are some other students in the department. I only recognize one of them, a girl in my Contemporary Russian Literature seminar, who is studying Russian because she says she wants to work for the CIA, which actually appears on her résumé, so the gossip goes, as Career Objective.

My party is a moderate success. There is good

vodka and a nice selection of Russian and American fingertip food: potato chips, dip I whipped together with sour cream and a box of instant soup mix, fruit, cheese, a big stainless-steel bowl full of winter salad contributed by my favorite KGB agent, and some piroshki I made this morning. One of the writers from *Panorama*, the local Russian-language newspaper, has volunteered to provide the entertainment and is effectively driving the guests to the other side of the room with his Russian ballads.

There is a rap at the door, and Pencil Neck lets himself in. He has a date after all—not Amy and not Kathy. She is dressed curiously, in a black skirt with a slit going up one leg and a frilly white blouse.

"Serge!" Pencil Neck waves to me. I chugalug a little more Stoly, straighten my ascot (I have on the pink-and-green silk one from Hungary, the same one I was wearing the night I was arrested after the Writers Union reading of *Trespassers Welcome Here*), and meander my way over.

"This is Vicky," he says, trying to be blasé, when in truth he looks like the cat who eats the canary.

Her face is flat and pretty in the basic American way. There is a rectangular piece of white plastic pinned to her chest. A name tag.

"Icky?" I ask, reading the tag.

"Vicky, Vicky!" Pencil Neck yelps over the balladeer. "The *V* fell off."

"I knew I should have changed before I came," apologizes Icky.

Pencil Neck plucks her name tag off her chest and puts it on mine. "Now you're Icky," he says.

"I work at Salty Dogs in Santa Monica. They make us dress up like ships' wenches. I know it's sexist, but I'm saving for a trip to Europe."

"What is ship's wench, Icky?"

She looks up at Pencil Neck and smiles with half her mouth. "You're right, he is cute."

"Hello, you two, glad you finally made it." It's Marina, sneaking up behind me before I've had time to formulate a plan. She takes Vicky by the arm and, as she leads her away to the buffet table, whispers in my ear. "Vicky is also guilty of reading the seditious *Point of Pride*, Sergei Pavlovich."

"And now I will sing a popular tune by Aleksandr Galich," announces the balladeer. Somewhere, someone has turned on a radio.

Claire Davis has left her subordinate spot on the floor and is looking through a picture book of the Crimea with a dissident sculptor whom I knew in Moscow.

"Claire Davis, I must speak with you."

"Listen, Sergei: *Ne stree yaitsee.*" Her cheeks are flushed from the Stoly. She is a master at acting as though nothing has happened.

"It means don't shoot," the sculptor chimes in. "A very important thing to know these days, a very important thing to know."

"Who told you about that book?" I whisper. I sit down opposite her on the coffee table, on top of the line of magazines I arrange every morning as a ritual before I sit down to write, one on top of the other like long, thin steps. The *Atlantic*, *The New Yorker*, *People*, *Playboy*. I sweep them onto the floor and sit back down. The glass is cool through my jogging suit.

"This book?" She holds up the book of the Crimea.

"No, no, the . . . that, the Gennady Blizitsky book."

"Oh, that. I already finished it. Yawn city."

"At least it was short." It's my darling KGB,

back with a plate full of goodies. She folds herself onto the couch next to the sculptor. "The piroshki are delicious, Sergei Pavlovich."

"Why did you assign that book?"

"What?" Marina cocks her head and delicately places a potato chip on her tongue.

"That book! Don't insult my intelligence. Anyone who has knowledge of my history would not even mention that book or that author in my presence, much less assign it for entire class to read."

Marina swallows deliberately and wipes one corner of her mouth with the pad of a ring finger. "I'm sorry, but the department chairman did not mention to me that our reading list had to agree with your personal history."

"It is not just my personal history, Marina. It is our collective history—the collective history of half the people in this room. *Point of Pride* is a piece of revisionist claptrap, an attempt to prevent the sins of the fathers from visiting the children by redefining the sins as . . . as bad habits!"

I am shrieking. I am drawing attention to myself. Even the long-playing balladeer has been distracted. Claire Davis is looking up from her picture book. She stares at me in that ironic, amused, uneasy way in which Americans regard people preaching Jesus on the street or bag folk shaking their fists at invisible enemies; it is an expression reserved for people who talk to themselves.

"That is interesting," says Marina. "Some people say your work is sanctimonious Westernizing claptrap."

"Who says that? Gennady Blizitsky and who else?"

"But I look at it like this. If I have a choice between trying to teach ninety-seven pages of revisionist claptrap or four hundred sixty-seven pages—your latest book is four hundred sixty-seven pages long, isn't it?—of sanctimonious Westernizing claptrap, I'll choose the ninety-seven-page version. Have you ever tried teaching modern Soviet literature to students who won't even read American literature?"

"And what does KGB have to say about this?" I ask.

I have not made an accusation, but she knows what I'm saying. Even though we have been speaking English, I expect to be chastised and dismissed in wordless Russian. I expect to be frozen with a stare as cold as my Stoly.

Instead she is overcome by short, breathless barks. Tears wiggle off the pink bottom ledge of her eyelids. I have seen her laugh before like this only once, at a Polish joke Pencil Neck shared in the office. Finally, she leans over very close to me and says, in a Russian accent that one hears only in American spy movies, "I cannot imagine what ze KGB would say, Comrade, but I am sure zat if zey knew my position, zey would think I was beink very, how do you say, realistic."

Vodka dredges up old memories. As I sit by the side of the pool, floating my bottle of Stoly on the surface, I remember the night Gennady Blizitsky and I read portions of *Trespassers Welcome Here* aloud at the Writers Union. It was standing room only, and from where I sat at a long wooden table at the front of the room, I heard whisperings that there was a line of people five blocks long waiting to get in. (Were they waiting to hear us, Gennady Ilyich, or *Trespassers?* I've often wondered.)

"Hey, Sergei," Gennady whispered over at me, "see the one in the gray tweed coat?" He pointed to a tall brunette standing just inside the door. "She wanted to see you so bad she traded her blue jeans right off her body." In those days he had standard horn-rimmed glasses, no wire-rims, and looked like a blond Buddy Holly.

I followed the end of his finger and saw that, indeed, the girl had her coat wrapped tightly around her, and her bright white legs were stockingless, her feet shoved into a pair of scuffed-up black wooden clogs.

"No kidding," I said. This was not an unlikely thing to happen then, people trading the clothes right off their backs to attend a literary reading. I strained to follow her as she moved through the crowd, looking for a seat. When she finally sat down, her coat fell open and I saw she was wearing a blue turtleneck and a brown skirt, just like hundreds of other young women you see around Moscow every day.

I looked over and expected to see Gennady laughing, one friend teasing another, but his face was closed, his smile curdled. "You are so gullible," he said, "I sometimes don't know how you manage."

One week later, he was claiming to be the gullible one. Through humble tears, he denounced me and *Trespassers Welcome Here* on a national radio broadcast. I was soon sharing a jail cell with a rabbi, who taught me the American verb "to be sold down river."

My thoughts are interrupted by Pencil Neck, who lurches out of the apartment and toward the pool. "What's wrong with you? You're supposed to be celebrating. You're an American now."

"Only because I'm a no-man." I push the bottle with the toe of my tennis shoe. It bobs away slowly. Someone has thrown a small metal table into the pool. It has drifted down to the bottom next to the lounge chair. A perfect place to finish the evening, I think.

"A no-man? Is that something Russian?"

"If I was not a no-man, I would be in Moscow this very day."

"What are you talking about? This is your party. Don't get morose on me."

"It's the opposite of a yes-man, *da?* If I was a yes-man, I would be in Moscow right now. There would be people who find my work . . . to have meaning. There would be Boris."

"A no-man—are you sure about that? You sure we're not talking nomad?"

"It's so obvious."

Pencil Neck whoops with delight and nearly crashes over into the swimming pool. "A no-man! I finally got you—there's no such thing! Hey, Vicky, you gotta hear this one!" He runs back into the apartment.

My Stoly is marooned in the middle of the pool now. It is quite lovely, reflecting the light the way a clear Christmas ornament reflects lights on the tree. I can see in the apartment that most of the food on the buffet table is gone. Claire Davis and Icky are singing along with the radio, using salt and pepper shakers for microphones.

I decide it is time to investigate the lounge chair. I take off my tennis shoes and, before plunging in, remove my ascot. It has been through so much already.

# DISARMING BIG MAD

## CLAIRE DAVIS

My mother, Big Mad, collects firearms, unusual people, and legends about herself. She likes to clean her guns over after-dinner coffee and Cointreau, and one night when I stuck around to witness the ritual, she came up with this harbor cruise idea. Dad had wisely excused himself and vanished. I sat watching her poke an old bit of one of my flannel nightgowns through the chambers of her Colt .45.

"Somewhat sexy," she said. "How can somebody be somewhat sexy?"

I had been telling her about Serge, the current writer in residence at the Department of Slavic Languages and Literatures, where I'm the secretary. I told about his expulsion from the Soviet Union for bringing out a scandalous book of essays, about his Guggenheim, about his being somewhat sexy. As soon as this last word slipped out of my mouth, I knew it was ammunition.

"I don't know," I said. "Vera—you know, the department chair?—she said he was a real ladies' man back in Moscow."

"A ladies' man? This is the same fellow who wears a black jogging suit and a black ascot for formal occasions?" She picked up the Colt and, squinting an auburn-lashed eye, looked over the sight at a Weight Watchers recipe pinned to the refrigerator by a magnet.

"He doesn't do that anymore; only when he first got here."

"Well, then, what does he do, hm? What makes him so somewhat sexy?" Her green eyes widened, dark and round as unripe grapes. She enjoys thinking I lead a wild secret life.

"Oh, Mom." I stood up and took the coffee cups to the sink.

"Why don't you ask this Sergei down to the boat for the day?" She says Sergei to rhyme with clergy. "I'd love to meet him, and I'm sure he'd get a kick out of it. Has he seen the ocean yet?"

"Mother, he's been in L.A. for six months."

"Bring him, and that teaching assistant you've told me so much about—the one who reminds you of Barbara Walters. Bella Bogoga. And her funny husband—what's his name? Fuzz?"

"*Yuz.*"

"Don't get upset, honey. I'm just teasing."

Part of my job as the department secretary is to take Serge around. We've spent hours traveling the freeway: finding him a place to live, tracking down a good Russian bakery, sending manuscript pages to his publisher in New York.

Two Tuesdays before the date set for the harbor cruise, we were on a quest for some Lacoste shirts to send back to his twenty-year-old son, Boris, whom Serge was forced to leave in the Soviet Union. Driving to the freeway, we passed the wholesale furniture outlet, which Serge claims looks straight from downtown Moscow.

On the cinder-block wall facing the freeway, furniture is advertised as FORNITURE in chartreuse letters eight feet tall. On the sidewalk in front of the store, there are dozens of beanbag chairs piled one on top of the other, like bright plastic rolls of fat, and crushed-velvet sofas with matching love seats, and toilet seat covers. A limp mattress has been suspended over the entrance for as long as Serge and I have been running errands together, and a hand-lettered sign is pinned to it: HELP CELEBRATE THE OLYMPICS! OLYMPIC MATTRESS ONLY $29.99, $24.99, $19.99!

As we passed the outlet, Serge nodded his shaggy head toward the mattress. "What would you give me to go in and buy that right here and now on the spot?"

"Less credit than I usually do," I said. "When I was in college, my roommate bought a mattress from one of these places and it turned into a taco every time she sat on it. Not only that, but there was this funny black stuff that seeped out from under the buttons and made her eyelashes fall out." Serge makes me nervous—for a Russian émigré writer that no one's ever heard of, he's pretty famous—and I always overdo the anecdotes. "What do you want to do with it, anyway?"

He took his eyes from the road long enough to make me a gift of a glance that I had heard from the other women in the department was infamous and lethal. "I want to share it with you."

He wants to *share* it with me? Serge once made a toast at a party he gave to celebrate his official emigration and said, "Up your ass!" instead of "Down the hatch!" and since then I get concerned that he doesn't always know what he's saying.

"You want to share it with me?" I said. "Isn't this a little advanced for you, Serge?" When in doubt, I buy time. Unfortunately I have a lot of time on my hands and not much else.

Big Mad would have predicted that my sarcasm was as good as a flat refusal, but he seemed to think it was funny. He chuckled a low, slow growl. "You mean you want me to say it the Russian way, huh? No monkeying around. Hey, Claire Davis, do you want to be my lover or not?"

There must be something wrong with me, because all I could think of when I heard this were the pictures he showed us after the department staff meeting last week. "Hey, everybody, do you want to see pictures of my boy Boris or not?" He tossed the photographs onto the middle of the table as if they were damning evidence. They were too blue and too dark, but you could see how the shadowy face hovering above the Bruce Springsteen T-shirt was exactly like the face of the father. And now, instead of responding to the yelp my body made at the mention of the word "lover," I remembered the serious face of Boris, self-consciously winking and thumbing his nose at the blurry gray onion domes of St. Basil's behind him.

Serge said nothing, and neither did I. I watched him light a cigarette and pull it from his lips between his middle and ring fingers like Boris must do, experimenting with ways to make smoking look natural. As he exhaled, he looked over at me, deep in the eyes, wise and a little sleazy, and I suddenly thought of the shards of gossip, the speculation. Once I had heard Vera call him the Playboy of the Eastern Bloc; someone else had observed that his lips were so red they were obscene. Another professor, who allegedly knew from experience, confirmed that what you've always heard about men with thick fingers is true.

My eyes strayed to where his hands gripped the steering wheel. It hit me then that a man over forty could be something else besides someone else's dad.

The Saturday of the harbor cruise is one of those dry, sharp days that people move to California for. The smog is almost unnoticeable, just a hazy band of beige edging the horizon, and everything within a fifty-mile radius of the marina that floats is out. Couples career past on Hobie Cats, weekend sailors motor out to sea on sailboats with fast lines and too much chrome, well-meaning fathers and their reluctant sons hunch over together in small gray rowboats, attempting to fish.

When Serge and I arrive, Dad is at the helm of the *Valhalla*, with his head cocked, listening to the health of the engines. Big Mad is setting out Triscuits and her famous liver pâté. Bella and Yuz are nowhere to be seen.

Suddenly there is the sound of heels clacking down the dock, and we all look up to see Bella rushing toward us in a pair of white platform shoes that could only look normal on a female impersonator.

Serge once commented, before he got his American colloquialisms ironed out, that he and Bella were like cats and dogs in oil and water. Bella is the oldest teaching assistant in the Slavic Department and still hasn't figured out that she is a graduate student first, a teaching assistant second. She's failed her Old Church Slavonic class once, and Serge's class, a graduate seminar in contemporary Russian émigré literature, twice. She claims it's impossible for her to learn anything from someone who's been in Los Angeles even less time than she has.

"Yuz is sorry he cannot come," says Bella. "He had to go to heart doctor. Sorry to be late."

"He's all right, isn't he?" I ask.

"Sure. Testing only he goes for today. I am late because I have to stop for the white pants." She taps her fingertips on her thighs. The pants are about five inches too long. Her murder-red toenails peep out from under the hem.

"White pants?" says Serge. "We are sitting here growing moss on ourselves waiting for you, and you are out shopping for white pants?"

For a few minutes they go at it in Russian.

Suddenly Serge falls into his deep growling laugh. Bella purses her lips, and the parts of her cheeks that frame her heavy dots of rouge redden. "And I suppose you never make any mistakes, Mr. Big Shot?"

Serge wipes his eyes with the back of his hand. "She thought you were not allowed on a yacht in this country unless you wore all white."

"I don't understand," says Big Mad, smiling. She happily suspects that Russians are indecipherable. "She thought you weren't . . ."

"It's tennis!" Serge cries. He is laughing so hard I think he's going to choke.

"I know that now, Mr. S.O.B., and I am terribly sorry in my heart for having wasted all your time." Bella prides herself on knowing all the social customs of the American bourgeoisie. Her eyes are red with tears.

"Oh, Bella, forget him." Big Mad flaps her hand

at Serge. "Let's just get rolling. I make a mean vodka martini. And I know you people can't resist anything with vodka in it, can you?"

As we leave the harbor for the ocean, we cruise past another fishing trawler, just like ours. There is a woman sitting on deck wearing bifocals and knitting a sweater too warm for this southern climate. She looks up at us as we pass. She stares. I wonder what she sees, how she puts us together.

Dad must be easy to figure out: the *Valhalla* is his child. He's spent three years restoring her, three years bent over in the sun, so the strait of skin running between the top of his T-shirt and his close-cropped white hair is baked brown as a California hill in August. He steers her gently, sipping his drink and tapping his foot to the Dixieland tape he's just slid into the tape deck. But what does she make of the rest of us? There's Bella Bogoga, with her frosted hair and molars so packed with gold that they glint in the sun when she laughs; Big Mad, already sunburned, her face ablaze with freckles, gesturing wildly with her martini glass and deep in the telling of one of her legends; Serge, in a tweed jacket and apricot-colored ascot, looking like a refugee from a late-night talk show; and me, sitting slightly apart from them all, mulling over the implications of Big Mad's wink.

When we came aboard this morning, she was already fixing martinis, bustling around the galley in the bell-pepper-green pantsuit that she treated herself to in celebration of the moon landing in 1969. Dad and I have been begging her for years to retire it, but she refuses, saying that she'll never be able to find another shade of green that so complements her red hair, which hasn't really been red since she was on the homecoming court at Kalamazoo High.

"I hope you're ready for some outlandish martinis," she had greeted us. "Sergei, you like martinis, don't you? Claire, that's a darling turtleneck—are those little hearts on it? Here, let me help you aboard." She reached toward Serge, fluttering the tips of her fingers.

"Mom, I got this turtleneck on sale at Robinson's. They have some great pantsuits—"

"Now don't get started on me about my pantsuit, Claire. Sergei, isn't this a wonderful shade of green?" She turns around for him. "It's hard for us redheads to find a good shade of green. You know—you have a little red in your hair." He has no red in his hair. "Plus, this is a—what's the word?"

"A relic," I said.

"A classic," she said. She tipped her head up and finally took a good look at Serge from over the tops of her freckled cheeks. "My, my, you're much handsomer than I thought you'd be."

"Yes. Really. Well." He tucked his fingers into the pockets of his jeans and rocked forward on the balls of his feet. He was actually embarrassed. The Playboy of the Eastern Bloc was embarrassed when Big Mad said the same thing to him that she's said to every boy I've ever brought home since Dennis Crosby in the first grade. It was unfair of her to make him look so predictable so quickly, but before I even knew I felt this, she winked at me. Suddenly I was an accomplice. This is Big Mad's specialty, capturing your allegiance before you realize you want to withhold it from her.

Big Mad first began winking at me on a regular basis when I was twelve years old. There was a boy in school, Kent Butterfield, whom I loved desperately, and one day during spring vacation Big Mad and I ran into him and his mother in the men's department of the Broadway.

This was the first shock. It was always assumed that boys like Kent Butterfield were exempt from the mundane, that when they weren't at school being cool, they were wrapped up in old, clean, soft diapers, like Big Mad's pearl-handled revolver, and stored away for safekeeping in a felt-lined box. Yet there he was. At the Broadway. With his mother. Pawing through three-packs of Fruit-of-the-Loom undershirts on sale.

"That's *him*," I hissed to Big Mad, from behind a rack of socks.

"Who?"

"*Him*. Kent Butterfield."

"Oh, *him*." Her voice flew up an octave in recognition. She sidled over to see what Butterfield mother and son were purchasing. She peeked over Mrs. Butterfield's shoulder, then announced in her deep, loud voice: "Listen, my daughter and I were just over at J. C. Penney's, and they're having a sale on athletic supporters, half price."

And then she winked at me.

There we were, just she and me, ruining my life together. However, Mrs. Butterfield didn't help things out either. She turned to Big Mad and said, like it was the most normal thing: "Why, thank you— *he really goes through them*, you know."

I tilt my head back and look up at the sun through my eyelashes. It's hot, and I feel drowsy and stupid. We are several miles out to sea, and another boat, called *The Bearded Clam*, floats by. A pair of identical twins wearing sun visors heave a bulging green plastic garbage bag over the side.

"The Doublemint Twins," says Serge.

"You know, on Rodeo Drive you can buy designer guns," I hear Bella say. "They are fourteen-carat gold or something and with diamonds in the trigger."

"Really. Now, that's something worth looking into, isn't it, Alek?" says Big Mad.

"Sure is, Babe." Dad nods his head to the beat of the Dixieland.

Big Mad is telling the legend of how she came to own seventeen guns. Dad collects them too. I grew up with a World War II submachine gun propped in the corner of the guest bathroom and a Remington rifle snuggled in the fold-out couch. One day he decided to put the guns to use and took one of those firearm training seminars held at the police department. Big Mad tagged along, and as the legend goes, she was the only one of the three women there who could fire a .357 Magnum without flinching.

"You know what a Magnum is, don't you?" she asked Bella.

"Dirty Harry," says Serge. He lights a cigarette and flips the match overboard.

"She is asking me," says Bella.

"They had us using bleach bottles full of water for targets. The bullet of a Magnum doesn't just make a hole, no—the whole damn thing explodes. Then we had an exercise where we fired at a mattress with a black burglar painted on it. I fired so consistently that I made a big hole right through the mattress." She neglects to say that the hole was through the elbow.

Bella's eyes are wide. "You shoot at black people?"

Serge chuckles, and Bella shoots him a nasty

glare. "No, it was a black painting," he says, "a silhouette meant to represent a burglar."

"I know what a silhouette is, Cookie," says Bella.

Big Mad smiles from one to the other; she hasn't
even had to instigate this. "Tell me, how long have
you known each other—did you know each other before you came here?"

"Of course," says Bella. "What do you think?
We work together in Russian Department."

"I think she was referring to Soviet Union,
Cookie," Serge says.

Bella smiles at him, sweet and evil. "Oh, yes,
Madeleine," she says. "As a matter of fact, my best
friend's cousin's sister Dunya knew this very same
Sergei Pavlovich one summer at Crimea Sea."

Serge has been idly watching the garbage bag
roll among the waves, but at the mention of Dunya
and the Crimea, his head snaps around.

"The Crimea. It sounds so romantic. Was it romantic?" Big Mad fishes around in her martini glass
for her olive and pops it into her mouth. She smiles,
girlish and disarming. She looks like a kid with a
jawbreaker stuck in her cheek.

"Ask Roosevelt," Dad says.

"Ask Stalin!" I say. Silence and dirty looks from
everyone. Serge doesn't see that I'm trying to help
him. "Actually, Sergei Pavlovich was there at some
writers' meeting, weren't you?"

"I was visiting a colleague in Simferopol and
also presenting a paper. It was a nice time. It is like
this a little, but the sky is more blue, not like the
dust clouds you find underneath the sofa."

"Was Dunya the colleague you were visiting,
then?"

"No, Dunya is a doctor," Bella says. "He met

her when he goes to the clinic for treatment on his
asthma."

"Claire, why didn't you tell me he had asthma?
Sergei, is my cigarette bothering you?"

"*My* cigarette isn't bothering me," he says.

"I didn't know he had asthma, Mom. You make
it sound like I know every detail about his life."

"Well, don't you?" says Big Mad, raising her
eyebrows.

"Of course not," I say.

"Yes, this Dunya was his doctor," Bella says
loudly, "and this Dunya was also a pretty girl who
he was making hanky-panky with in between her
shifts at the clinic."

"Hanky-Panky? Capital *h* hanky, capital *p*
panky?" Big Mad leans forward and raps Serge play-
fully on the knee. "What about this?"

If this were the Kent Butterfield episode, I
would be cringing behind the sock rack right about
now.

"She said it was like this. 'Bella Semyonovna,
you know that Mr. Big Shot writer Sergei Pavlovich?
Well, being in the bed with him is like pulling off a
Band-Aid. You close your eyes, you hold your breath,
there is a tiny pinch, and pfftt! Is all over!' " Bella
sits back daintily and steers a cracker heaped with
pâté into her mouth. She chews, swallows, and
smiles. Her molars flash in the sun.

Big Mad hoots so loud that a flock of sea gulls
feeding nearby scatter. "Oh, that can't be," she says.
"Look how handsome he is."

What he is, is mortified. His cheeks are the color
of the inside of a plum, but his face is impassive. His
lips are tight. It occurs to me that this is the face he
must have presented to the secret police during his
long interrogations.

Dad changes the subject before he hears something he suspects he doesn't want to know. "We're far enough out now—what do you say we have a little target practice? And could you set this old man up with another martooni?" He shakes the ice in his glass and deploys a benign smile in our general direction, being careful not to touch Serge with it. This is his way of restoring the peace.

Big Mad takes Dad's glass. "Anyone else?"

Serge tips his head back and finishes his drink in several short swallows. As he drinks, I notice the stubble on his Adam's apple, coarse stubble on skin callused from shaving twenty years? Thirty years? I think maybe he seems his age after all.

"Claire, have I showed you my new piece?" asks Big Mad, disappearing into the hold. Her voice is warm, and there is an edge of thrill in it, as though we shared this kind of thing all the time, like household hints.

I expect her to come back packing a holster or carrying a leather case. Instead she reappears with an armful of empty bleach bottles and a crooked, disbelieving grin. "I forgot," she says. "I had it on me." She digs into her pocket and pulls out an oak-handled automatic.

"I thought I told you, Claire, I had all the pockets deepened in my pantsuits so I could walk heavy all the time."

"For all your treacherous shopping expeditions to the Galleria," I mutter, low enough so no one else can hear.

"Oh, look!" Bella says. She sits forward in her chair with her hands at her chest, one cupped over the other, peering at the automatic as though it were a living thing. She hasn't expected a real gun to materialize, but she is a real Russian and knows that you have a better chance of survival if you play to the person in power. "Nice steel," she says.

"Are you all right?" I lean over and whisper to Serge.

"Yes, of course," he says crisply. His eyes fall on me briefly, cold and foreboding as a Siberian sky. I've made the mistake of acknowledging his humiliation.

"May I hold it?" asks Bella.

"Sure," says Big Mad. "Dry fire it. See how clean the action is."

"A dry fire," says Bella, mystified.

Big Mad holds out an imaginary gun and pulls her index finger. "Click click. No bullets."

"Click click," says Bella. "I think I would rather you to click click."

"All right," says Big Mad, taking the gun back. She carefully wipes Bella's fingerprints off on her sleeve.

"This has nothing to do with the army, does it?" says Bella. "Not to make a criticism or anything."

I look at Serge to see if he'll comment on this, but he isn't paying attention. He is pushing up the cuff of his coat, checking the time on his waterproof watch.

"Of course not," says Big Mad. "We're just going to do a little target practice."

"Who as target?" asks Bella. "Another silhouette?"

"What?" Big Mad takes the automatic and shoves in the magazine.

"With who as the target?"

"These." Big Mad tosses one of the empty bleach bottles over the side.

She turns to Dad and nods. He stabs the gas pedal, and we speed off. Big Mad and I are the only ones on our feet, and we stagger toward the stern. About twenty-five yards away, Dad cuts the engine. It's quiet. The bottle bobs among the waves, distinguishable only by its ice-white color.

"These are special exploding bullets. Alek makes them himself." Big Mad plants her sandaled feet firmly on deck and takes aim. "When you shoot" —she wrinkles her nose and squints over the sight— "your shoulders and your hands should make a perfect triangle." The gun wavers at the tip of the triangle. She fires.

We look out at the bleach bottle. It's gone. She giggles and blows the end of the gun like a hero in a western. It's only a coincidence, a change in the wind, but it seems as if her demure puff has sent a pungent whiff of gunpowder my way.

"You missed it, Babe."

Dad's right. He points out at the bottle, which had disappeared in the trough of a wave. It rolls over lazily, untouched.

Big Mad is silent for a moment. She smiles over at me. An idea has struck her, the possibility for a new legend.

"Well, here, Claire, you try it."

"Me?"

"I can't believe this. Alek is an expert marksman and I'm a near expert marksman and we've reared a daughter who's afraid of guns." Big Mad shakes her head in mock sorrow. "C'mon, honey, I've done so much for you—can't you just do this little thing for me?" She rolls her eyes, half-kidding, but if the plea works, then it isn't a joke.

"Boris is the same as you, Claire," says Serge. "I feel I have done so much for him, yet he is never one to reciprocate."

"I reciprocate," I say indignantly.

"Claire didn't tell me you had a son, Sergei," says Big Mad.

"It seems that to get your children to do what you want, you have to ask them to do the opposite. But often if you ask them to do the opposite, they'll do what you ask and not what you want. Which is, I guess, the opposite of the opposite." He rubs his eyes.

"It's the same all over," says Bella, who has no children.

We are all quiet for a moment. A speedboat painted magenta and neon blue bobs by. There are three people in it, all trying to see through one pair of binoculars. "It's a whale!" one of them screeches. "No, it's just a bag of garbage," the one holding the binoculars confirms. I think they are looking at us.

"Just shoot the gun," says Serge. He closes his eyes and nods slightly.

There must be something wrong with me, because instead of seeing that he's just trying to prevent more feuding, I see him with Boris. I see him in the same tweed jacket, shopping with Boris in the giant G.U.M. store in Moscow; counseling him on the unknowable ways of women; sitting hunched over with him in a boat, fishing. I see him closing his eyes, this big Soviet dissident, and telling his son to do what he's told.

The idea of the Olympic mattress seems so stupid I can feel myself blush.

"Maybe she's afraid you'll find her unfeminine," says Big Mad, winking at Serge. He is now her ally, her comrade in child rearing.

I take the gun.

The bottle has drifted farther away, but it's still within range. I straighten my arm out and look down over my shoulder and out over my thumb. I will never hit it. I'll miss once, twice, maybe Big Mad will coerce me into firing an entire magazine, missing every time. The new legend will feature her and Serge and the moral that try as they might, children can never, will never, please their parents.

Then I get an idea. I think about it in an abstract way, but it's such an easy thing to do I don't have to muster up any real courage.

I open my hand quickly, spreading and extending my fingers, and Big Mad's oak-handled baby disappears into the sea.

"Claire! My God!" Dad rushes from the helm and looks overboard. "What happened? Are you all right?" Three brown lines crease his forehead. He probably thinks I've had a seizure or something.

"I'm fine," I say.

"What happened?"

"Nothing. I dropped it."

Bella stands up and joins Dad where he is still gaping over the side. They stare into the waves as though the automatic will resurface at any moment, like a porpoise.

"So in life there are small favors," says Bella. "It could have been one of those designer guns, and they are worth very many moneys."

Serge stands up and looks overboard too. He lights a cigarette and pulls a stray bit of tobacco off his tongue with his thumbnail. He is smiling, amused at this turn of events, but he's gone the way of Kent Butterfield, and even his lethal smile can't do much to recapture the old mystique.

Suddenly I feel the heel of a hand across my back. I turn to see Big Mad rubbing her wrist. It's red from where she's struck me. Physical punishment has never been her forte. She digs her fists into her hips.

"This is very funny, Claire. What do you do for an encore?"

I look right into her angry freckled face and wink.

# DEATH BY BROWSING

## BELLA BOGOGA

Last Saturday my husband Yuz collapsed in front of the Bullock's Wilshire department store in Los Angeles, California.

Forever I will see him falling against the palm tree, sliding down, down, his golf shirt bunching up under his arms, his poor bald head so sunburnt, his scattered few hairs stiff from sunscreen oil. I think of those frail hairs and cry.

I left him in the palm's stingy shade to rest and went for help. On my return, I found strangers buzzing over him, wondering about lawsuits and who should touch him. A man in a khaki safari shirt said, "The Russians! Such a beleaguered race!" This happened on the four-month anniversary of our departure from Moscow.

More difficult than deciding the fate of Yuz's ashes is writing to my friend Lidia Nikolaevna about

his death. For the moment, I keep his urn in a shoebox in the closet (former home of an adorable pair
of moss-green pumps) and spend the warm winter
evenings on my shoebox-sized balcony, ripping up
letter after letter to Lidia. Finally, afraid she might
hear of it through friends of friends of the nitwits I
work with at Slavic Languages Department, I manage to write:

2 February

Greetings, Cookie!
I have some horrible sad news. First, I could not
find that black-and-white Norma Kamali T-shirt
dress you asked me about in your last letter. Also,
dear Yuz died three weeks ago Sunday.
Los Angeles is perfect except the air and it
caused him to suffer a heart attack while shopping
on Wilshire Boulevard. The man on the news that
morning had said, "Beware. Third-stage smog alert.
Breathe only when necessary." But they always say
that, and you have to live, right? I did not realize it
was eight miles to walk to Bullock's Half-Year
Sale, and who could have known the bad state of
Yuz's heart? Months before, he had modern
hospital tests which said he was okay. The
emergency ward doctors felt that decades of vodka
tormenting his system were probably to blame.
It is no secret that my love for Yuz expired long
ago, but he was my husband, and the people at the
university allowed me time away to heal. It was
fantastic. Every day I spent visiting my friend
Cricket, darling salesgirl of Trendsetter Sportswear
at fancy downtown department store. You would
love her, Lidichka! She is Miss Au Courant,
straight from *Vogue*. With her tiny waist and saucy
hairstyle, she reminds me of you, only she is dark-
eyed like an Armenian. She admires greatly my
style of dressing and often asks my opinion on how

to put together a Look. She says I have natural
gifts for fashion and should be In Retail (as
salesgirl or clothes buyer) instead of teaching
Russian to college students.

I would appreciate if you kept the situation of
Yuz to yourself, as all those nasty black-market
girls, Irina especially, who tries to pass her cheap
Polish lipstick off for Revlon, will be delighted to
hear of my misfortune.

All my love,
Bella

16 March

Bellinka *doushka:*
I am *crushed* to hear what California has done to
our sweet Yuz! I think of you stranded there with
no one and nothing and I weep, Bella Semyonovna,
weep. Masha—you remember, the gymnast who
bought the HAWAII towel from you last spring?—she
just returned from a gymnastics exhibition in San
Jose, California, and said there is a mass murderer
going around Los Angeles. So what else is news, I
thought!

I couldn't help but tell Irina about Yuz. She *was*
upset and not nasty at all. Those girls love and
miss you, Bellinka. (They have me for all their
high-fashion needs, but who to get sunglasses from
now that you're gone?) Please keep well and keep
your door locked. Mass murderers especially
prefer women alone, you know. When you think
about it, could you check for the Norma Kamali in
blue and white?

Kisses,
Lidia

I answer this by folding it in thirds and placing
it under the short leg of the kitchen table to stop the
wobble. *What California has done to our sweet Yuz!*

I can just see Lidia's eyes glittering with pity. What a relief! Life in emigration *is* worse than Soviet Union.

The fact is, she is Miss Jealous.

Last summer, back in Soviet Union, when we did our rounds on Kalinin Prospekt, Lidia selling the sharpest illegal shoes in Moscow, me moving vacation apparel from a Samsonite briefcase I found on the metro, we debated our favorite topic: how we would live in the West. If I said I wanted to work in a clothes boutique, Lidia wanted to own one. If I wanted to be a *Vogue* photographer, Lidia would be the model I photographed. If I, exasperated, said I wanted to own *Vogue*, Lidia hiked up a lovely shell-pink nostril in disdain. "You're so *ambitious*, Bella. I'd rather live a simple life, having many children."

All this time, I never told her that Yuz, with his modest dream of picking lemons off his own tree in California, had changed our last name from Bogoga to Bogogowicz and was petitioning for emigration papers with a yarmulke on his head, fashioned from the cup of one of my black-market bathing suit tops.

The day the papers came through, I found Lidia on Kalinin Prospekt seducing a pigeon-toed clerical worker with a pair of Avia aerobics shoes. "Lidia, listen: Yuz has gotten—you won't believe it—we are leaving for United States."

She slowly turned. Her light-eyed gaze crashed down on me. "America, oi. When *I* emigrate, I'm going to Paris."

One day I come across Yuz's glasses under the nightstand. Without tears I suffered his cremation and a visit to the Foundling Home for the Children of Estonia, Westside Branch, where I donated his few clothes. But the glasses, the glasses, Yuz's most needed thing. I try to throw them away under the sink, then throw them off the balcony, which overlooks a Dumpster in the apartment building's parking lot. But I end by crawling through the garbage to retrieve them. I kiss them and place them in the shoebox, beside his urn. I realize it is time to bury him.

My fellow teaching assistants, all well-meaning émigré ladies with the fashion sense of potato farmers, suggest trying "Crypts" in yellow pages, or calling a little-known Russian actor/pilot who makes his living distributing ashes over the Pacific.

"What about Children of Estonia?" asks Valeria, dressed in black wool so old it's beginning to turn green.

Valeria, Marina, and I are in the office of the Slavic Languages Department, standing before Mr. Coffee pot, waiting for him to finish brewing our morning cup.

"Heavens to Bessie, no," I say. "They already have enough of him, all his nice slacks."

"Well, they were most helpful in finding me lawyer—a lawyer—for my divorce proceedings," says Valeria.

"Maybe under a lemon tree," I say suddenly. "Yes! To honor dream that brings him to this marvelous land."

"So marvelous," says the imperious Marina, "that if you attempted to bury the urn in a lemon orchard they would lock you away in prison. There are laws forbidding it, Bella."

"I will buy my own tree, then."

"I can just see it," says Marina, sipping on her coffee, winking at Valeria through the steam, "growing right in the middle of your lovely apartment."

I go to a discount nursery and find a potted tree still too young for fruit. I squeeze it onto the balcony. Inside of a week, the sun turns the leaves brown. In the evening, while I wait for news to be over and television to begin, I snap off the crisp, dead curls and miss the good side of Lidia Nikolaevna, which believes, on principle, that crazy ideas are the best kind.

I go to Trendsetter Sportswear, not to bother Cricket but to see if she has suggestions on a nice gift. I have never answered Lidia's condolence letter, and rather than apologize, I will find some luscious department store item to give to Jim Spaniel to take to Moscow to give to Lidia. Jim Spaniel is an assistant professor in the department, who takes, every summer, some Russian majors to Soviet Union. He is no big hunk, Jim, and his hairline has tiptoed back at least an inch in the few months I have known him, but he appreciates a good conversation and does not tease me about my fashion awareness.

On this day, one of Cricket's co-workers sees me before I even get off the escalator. She is tall and wrinkled, a permanent frown embedded in her saddle face. I wave to her, but she just looks back down at the rack of blouses she is straightening.

"Cricket has gone to lunch," she calls out.

"All right. I will just browse, then."

Cricket never comes, and I wander downstairs, where I find *the* item: soft caramel in color, soft as a baby's earlobe to touch, it is the most fantastic handbag I have ever seen. Unfortunately, it is hanging off the shoulder of a teenage girl with the haircut of an army officer. Mother, she calls, come here. She replaces the bag on top of a pile of other bags, all marked down from full price, her paw resting on the flap, staking it out for her own. But I *must* have it. I can just see it swinging down Kalinin Prospekt on Lidia's delicate shoulder. I can just see Irina and the rest of the black-market girls purring and stroking it like a talisman. Oh, to live in Los Angeles like Bella, they'll say.

The handbag will be trickier to capture when mother gets involved. I reach deep into the pile until cool leather nudges my armpit. I root around until I find a strap, then pull. The teenager screeches as an avalanche of navy-blue, bone, and dove-gray handbags cascades down on her feet.

The salesgirl comes and asks would I like the handbag cash or charge.

During the summer, I do not have to teach and am free to spend my days in the cool concrete wombs of my favorite department stores. I often stop downtown to visit Cricket but am always interrupting her at something: waiting on customers, clearing out dressing rooms, cleaning mirrors.

At home, I have managed to fit a stool on the balcony next to the lemon tree, and in the evenings I sit and work on my clippings file. With some money left from Yuz, I purchased subscriptions to *Elle, Glamour, Mademoiselle*, of course *Vogue*, and others, and I keep a file of valuable articles on, to give example, "Plaids: The Ultimate Mix and Match Challenge." I do not sit outside on Tuesdays, however, the evening before garbage pickup, because the Dumpster flies are too bothersome.

Sometimes I imagine Jim Spaniel and Lidia, together in Moscow at that very moment. I imagine him presenting her with the handbag, shyly, because

he is undone by her pale, cat beauty, and Lidia saying oh-oh-oh, taking the bag to her breast, stroking
it, inhaling the odor of real leather.

In early August, Jim Spaniel calls and invites
me out to take a beer. In honor of his return, I wear
my new melon-colored cotton twill skirt with royal-
purple top-stitching, which I had been saving for the
first day of class. With my bolero jacket and new
lace-up gladiator sandals, I plan on being a sight for
eyes sore from looking at frumpy Russian women all
summer.

Of course, I say it's wonderful. I tell him he is
the luckiest boy in the world. He smiles idiotically
and tears his cocktail napkin into strips. He is thin-
ner than I remember and, unlike every other person
in Los Angeles, hasn't a hint of suntan. In fact,
his skin is the color of mushrooms, no doubt from
making love all day in the bad air of Lidia's stuffy
apartment.

"She's a great lady," he breathes.

"Oh, yes, Cookie, she is fantastic. She is my
dearest friend. And so beautiful, really like an American beauty!"

"Oh, no, she's typically Slavic. That's what
makes her so unique."

"Yes, Cookie, unique as the two hundred fifty
million other Russians in the world. When is the
wedding?"

He tells me a date. He says it will be in Moscow.

On my way home on the bus—that lovelorn im-
becile doesn't even offer me a ride—I get off two
stops early and buy some plant food and a half gal-
lon of rum raisin ice cream.

When I was able, finally, to ask about the hand-

bag, he looked blank at me for a minute, as though
he'd forgotten. "Oh, right," he said. "She enjoyed it
very much."

"Did she love it?"

"Sure. You know how excited she gets. The
smallest thing sends her into orbit."

19 August

Dear Lidichka:
    What fantastic news I hear from your fiancé, a
certain Mr. Jim Spaniel. Jim is my favorite person
in the Slavic Department, and we are great friends.
As soon as he returned from Moscow he called me,
and we Did the Town, celebrating your happy
news. When, Lidichka, are you coming to Los
Angeles? It is a fabulous town. I will mention you
to Cricket (she is a darling, offering me such
compliments when I emerge from my dressing
room, whirling and twirling like a dancer from the
Kirov), but she may not immediately be able to see
us. Retail is a very competitive business, and she
has a very busy and erratic schedule. Not to be
disappointed, you'll have me and my Los Angeles
expertise. Oh, I nearly forgot, did you enjoy the
handbag? Just a trifle from yours truly.

All my love,
Bella


    Jim Spaniel insists on meeting Lidia at the air-
port alone. I try to arrange for champagne and a telegram singer, but he says absolutely not. I think he is
envious of my panache.
    Several days after her arrival, Lidia and I finally
rendezvous at Santa Monica Mall. We cover each
other's faces with kisses. Mascara tears of joy drib-
ble out from under Lidia's sunglasses.

"Are you sure you want to go shopping?" I say. "It looks like you've already been." I had expected her in her drab Moscow best; instead she is wearing a gorgeous red-and-white-striped sundress of Irish linen, cinched at the waist with a wide red leather belt.

"A present from Jim. Luckily, he is sturdier than Yuz. We must have been to every store in the city."

"And you purchased at full price?"

She shrugs. "Jim makes big money. He can afford nice things for his wife."

"He doesn't make so much money."

"Well, he must make more than you, Bellinka, and you're doing so well yourself. And look, you're wearing that fantastic dress! I almost didn't remember. You know, something like that would *sag* on me, but you fill it out so nicely." She shakes her head. Her butter-yellow curls erupt in a brand-new perm.

Stupidly, I chose for this special reunion a sentimental favorite, the polyester green-and-orange plaid A-line with contrasting yoke and pockets. I wanted Lidia to feel at ease, not intimidated by my new American Look.

"It was the only thing ironed," I say.

"And those *shoes*." Suddenly she drops to her knees. She strokes the tips of my moss-green pumps, like a jeweler feasting on a rare stone. Shoppers entering the store stare down at her. She is almost knocked over by a reckless mother and a baby stroller. But she sees none of it. She also does not see that this old, honest gesture has saved me from pulling the belt from this fantastic dress which I fill out so nicely and strangling her.

"A friend of Irina's was looking for a shoe just like this," she whispers, "but it was impossible to find. My one order I could never fill."

"Cookie! Please! There are shoes like this all over city! These were marked down at Bullock's. Nobody wanted green, apparently."

"I can see why," she says, standing and rubbing at two round bruises of dirt on the bottom of her dress.

In the mornings, she comes to work with Jim Spaniel, wearing each day some breathtaking new ensemble. The department secretary calls her the Russian Grace Kelly. To pass the time, she eavesdrops on the secretary's phone conversations or flips through dusty copies of *Soviet Life*. I have offered to give her my already read copies of *Vogue*, *Glamour*, etc., but she refuses them, then goes out and buys the exact ones I've offered. She says she can't do the help-yourself quizzes with my answers always staring her in the face.

On weekends, when Jim Spaniel is doing lesson plans or watching football, we go shopping.

As we sit one Sunday in afternoon beach traffic, silent and bored as mannequins, Lidia pokes into the bag on the seat between us. We are driving in Jim Spaniel's convertible car and playing his cassette tape deck. "Returning these, Bellinka? Too small?" She pulls out some blue jeans and checks the tag. "Fourteen. I guess not."

"They fit perfect. The waist is even too big. I buy them downtown for thirty-three dollars and return them in Beverly Hills, where they are forty-five dollars."

"They can't be the same blue jean."

"They are."

"You are sure?"

"Every store in the city carries them—they are a popular brand."

"And the style is the same?"

"Lidichka, I have been doing this for months."

"Well, I've never heard about it."

In the store, at the department of Misses Casual Fashions, I get around the question of a receipt by telling the salesgirl, a freckled darling of no more than seventeen, that I bought the blue jeans on the same day I discovered I was pregnant with twins. "So you can understand how I would misplace it."

"Je-sus, twins!" exclaims the girl, ringing open the cash register.

"Yes, I was thinking perhaps of calling them Bella and Lidia if they are girls."

"We had twins in my high school. You won't believe *their* names. Raoul and Bertha Controla. Bertha Controla. Could you like die?"

"This is Lidia's kind of game," I tell Jim Spaniel one afternoon over tamales. He has invited me to lunch to discuss what Lidia has told him is her new career.

"Buying blouses on sale at one store and selling them back to another one at full price?"

"She also does shoes and lingerie," I say.

"Terrific. This all happens to be completely illegal. Does she know she can go to jail?" In a short-sleeved blue-striped shirt, his pale face corrugated with worry, Jim looks like an inmate himself. He says he has lost sleep during the past three weeks. In the morning he gives Lidia fifty dollars, and in the evening, when he comes home, she has hundreds of dollars' worth of clothing piled on the sofa. "I understand what she's going through," he says, reaching for a napkin to shred. "I'm no stranger to the problems of Soviet émigrés. The difficulties of adjusting to a new culture, dealing with Western decadence, the sudden availability of goods. I even realize that she misses her black-market involvement. But she can't behave this way. She's here now. This is L.A., not some Tashkent bazaar."

"I don't know. To me it seems she has gotten back in her personality the kick and sparkle she had in Moscow."

"You want kick and sparkle? This keeps up, I'll show her some kick and sparkle."

I tell Jim Spaniel I will talk to her. Instead I borrow his car one day after school and take her to the garment district downtown.

These big warehouses have no air-conditioning, and every outlet reeks of perfumed sweat and frying hamburgers from the snack bar. I prefer my stores tranquil: soothing music, thick carpeting, private dressing rooms. Lidia, however, was born for such a rough-and-tumble consumer workout as this. In one and a half hours, she emerges from Bob's Discount House of Polyester lugging four sweaters, a leather vest, five poly-blend blouses, and ten pairs of leather sandals from Milan. Her face is as radiant as a young mother bringing home her firstborn.

"Now where?" she chirps, as I steer the car from the parking lot. She leans down and helps her toes swiggle into a new sandal and buckles it. The buckle comes off in her hand. She shrugs and drops it out the window.

I suggest lunch. There are good burgers at Cassell's, greasy piroshki at Gorky's.

"Uff, it's too hot. How can you even think about food? I want to meet your friend Cricket. She works around here, doesn't she?"

"She is busy. She can't always talk."

"Let's go anyway. We can buy some Godiva chocolate."

As we enter Trendsetter Sportswear, I see Cricket standing behind the counter, folding bright cotton sweaters and talking on the phone. Her head is bent, the receiver clamped to her shoulder with the aid of her small, pointed chin. She is listening, and while she waits for her turn to talk, she mouths the words to a rock-and-roll song coming from a television mounted near the ceiling. The television portrays three singing boys in black leather driving motorcycles around Greek ruins.

Lidia stops halfway to the counter, diverted by some lovely cranberry-colored silk blouses. She flips through the rack wildly. "Bellinka," she says, "these blouses!"

Cricket looks up, startled. I wave to her. Despite the music and Lidia's chatter, I am close enough to hear her whisper into the receiver: "Oh, God, Molly, you won't believe who's here. The Russian pest."

I pretend to watch the boys on television. They hurl one of the motorcycles over a cliff. They sing: "You're a one-woman torture chamber, got my heart on the rack."

Cricket gets off the telephone. She knows I hear, so she becomes official. "If you ladies would like me to start a dressing room for you today, just let me know."

"I would like to return this blouse," says Lidia. As she approaches the counter, she pulls one of her cheap outlet blouses from her handbag. "See?"

"I can't do that," says Cricket.

"My receipt, I had it as bookmark in book which I returned to library."

"You didn't get that here. It's from Bob's Discount House of Polyester."

"No, is from here."

"I'm sorry, but I can't take anything back without a receipt."

"But I just explained about receipt. The book was overdue."

"Lidia, please," I finally say. "This is Cricket. You shouldn't give her a bad time."

"So this is our Cricket! I am Lidia Nikolaevna, Bella's friend from Moscow."

Cricket picks up the sweaters she was folding and hugs them to her chest. "Please leave. I can't help you."

"Then perhaps the question is how can I help you? At home I have lovely Calvin Klein blue jeans that look just your size. And a gorgeous pink sweater, hand-knitted from People's Republic of China. Hand-knitted, Cricketchka! Imagine how luxurious! It would look stunning on you, emphasize the nice figure. Make the boyfriend swoon. If you make a refund on this blouse, I fix you up with an entire outfit. You be czarina of the high school. Cricketchka. Crinketinka."

Cricket puts the sweaters down. Her eyes are averted, her shoulders stiff with discomfort and fear. She picks up the telephone and dials the department of security.

Two weeks later, the lemon tree looks better. I have learned the trick of not too much sunlight, not too much shade, not too much water, not too much dry. One night, I decide it's time to distribute Yuz's ashes. I retrieve his shoebox from the bottom of my closet. It is late, past the late movie, and I jump when the doorbell rings. It's Lidia. She has suitcases. She comes inside without saying hello and asks, "Can I come live with you?"

"If you do not mind some of Yuz's things still around."

"*Spasiba*, Bellinka." She stares down at the shoebox in my hand. She tilts her head to read the end of the box. "The moss-green pumps. My favorite."

"They are good shoes. Faithful. Come, I'll show you where to put your things."

I don't ask what happened with Jim Spaniel. After he came and straightened us out with the department store security officer, he stopped bringing Lidia to work with him. I assume he also displayed to her the threatened kick and sparkle.

I show her how to use the washing machine in the basement and make a space on the balcony for another chair. During the day she watches the television. During the night she sets the alarm so she can get up and talk long distance to Moscow. I never get around to Yuz's ashes. The shoebox sits on the kitchen counter under a stack of magazines.

One day I come home from the Bullock's Thanksgiving Pre-Sale, to find a note:

Bella *doushka:*
    My friend Arkady—you know, at *Pravda?*—he has pulled some strings and managed to get me back. I tried to call at the office but they said you were in class all day. I had to do it standby, so there was no time. Thank you for the past few weeks at your apartment. I hope you don't mind, I took those nice moss-green shoes. My lady who was looking for them will be ecstatic!

Love,
Lidia

I fold the note, then rip it in two. I sit down at the table, push back a cuticle with my thumbnail, pick some fuzz from the carpet. Strange. I notice that I am wearing my nice moss-green shoes.

Suddenly I see her, marching down Kalinin Prospekt. She searches out the old customer, pulls her into an empty street and, touching her lips to an ear already raw from Moscow cold, whispers, "This is *nothing* compared to the other shoes of Los Angeles," or, "Look, just for you!" then finally, slowly, lifts the lid off the box, only to discover that instead of pumps, she has in her possession an urn in basic black and a pair of Soviet spectacles.

Poor Yuz, I think. All that effort to emigrate.

From my balcony, I can dispose of the lemon tree. I make a little ceremony of it, then drop it into the Dumpster, where it lands with a *thook*.

# KEEP YOUR GUTS

## TANYA ZLOPAK

My last cattle call takes place on a smoggy day, temperature over one hundred degrees. Every just-starting-out actress in Los Angeles is there, all lined up, all trying for this part, the female lead in a movie directed by Solly Stein. Even I heard of this guy when I am actress in Moscow. He has big reputation for realism. In his last picture, rumor says, he spends over one hundred thousand dollars on authentic Victorian keyholes visible only in long shot.

Standing in front of me are two bony American beauties. One in a halter dress. All the sharp inside parts of her back can be seen from the outside. She is telling her friend about recent operation to enlarge her cheekbones. She tells how the skin under her eyes is slit open and pyramids of silicone tucked in. The friend says she has heard of times when these implants wander around the body. A woman she knew had a breast implant that wound up in her armpit. The girls look about twenty-two years old.

"Stop this!" I yell. "You guys are so gruesome!" I cover my ears with my hands.

Through my fingers I hear the cheekbone one say, "You do what you have to do."

Normally, I believe Los Angeles is not a bad place for Soviet émigrés—those from Moscow especially are used to sprawl and anonymity, and there is large émigré community here—but the heat and craziness can make you sick. I close my eyes. Sharp zots of color whiz around behind my eyelids. I only stay in line because I believe I have a chance. The advertisement said this role called for "a faded Russian beauty, sensual and world-weary." I am her.

Before I left Soviet Union, I am co-star of film called *I Traded My Love for a Barge*. The premise was this: Typical spirited Socialist heroine leaves husband and "self-satisfied" life in Moscow to help make quota at failing shipyards in Sevastopol.

Except for these idiotic movie roles, my Moscow life was not so bad. I was no dissident. Soviet Union had provided me a good education and career as medium-range actress. I had season hockey tickets and beautiful high-ceilinged apartment in old section of town, with new painted walls. The paint was gotten secretly from West Germany by my lover, Valentin. It was melted-sherbet color, this paint, a shade known as Innocent Peach. Valentin and I painted my walls together, then made love against them while they were cool and soft, barely dry. I talked Valentin's head blue about my love of Innocent Peach. You would think it safe, right? Talking to your lover about the color of your walls.

My role in this barge movie was as the lonely, well-groomed confidante who convinces our heroine to drop everything to go help the Motherland. It was a stupid, impossible piece of acting.

"No young wife leaves her husband to build boats in Sevastopol!" I shrieked at Valentin, who was also my director. Outside my apartment, we screamed at one another until our veins threatened to burst. We got into love only because each respected the other's work, but we were otherwise not well suited.

He told me to take it up with Central Script Editorial Administration. Until we received an official response from them, however, I was to put my arm around the heroine's shoulder and sing, sotto voce, the "Internationale" into her ear. I would not. Valentin was furious. I was doing this to him always, he said, trying to Westernize my role. In a fit, he communicated my insolence to those responsible for tapping telephones and breaking car windshields.

I visited a friend's dacha just outside Moscow for two days, hoping to get my mind away. When I arrive back Monday, what do you think I found? No telephone tap. No broken car windshield. No one even trails me. But they had painted my walls. Such trouble they go to. They had broken in and covered Innocent Peach with a mucous brown, color of the glistening muck left behind by snails.

I saw Valentin once more before I left. Our barge movie was complete, and won many awards at Tashkent Film Festival. The awards turned him sweet. He said beauty of my acting raised tears to his eyes every time he saw the picture. I hold no grudges against Valentin. Is impossible not to love a little the person who loves what you create.

At open cattle calls you read for casting director or even assistant casting director. Some harassed-

looking girl with big eyeglass frames. But this Solly
Stein, he is particular: he wants to see us himself. He arrives perfectly at ten o'clock, driving a
sea-green Rolls-Royce. The license plate says REEL.
His eyes, I noticed, matched perfectly the color of
his car.

The reputation of Solly Stein says he is fat, big-
hearted, and meticulous. In truth, he is some form
of modern-day holy. I have not had any acting job
since I came to Los Angeles one year ago. I have no
agent. I have not membership in SAG, AFTRA, those
suspiciously initialed, closed organizations to which
you must belong to get paying acting jobs. I go only
to open cattle calls. Commercials for cold medicine,
breakfast cereals. Outer-space pictures in need of exotic alien beauties. I tried, along with eight hundred
others, for role of International Tampax Spokes-
woman. Just for experience, I took a job as a corpse
in a student film production. I was fired when the
nineteen-year-old director said I looked too old dead.
He said my face sagged when I lay on my side. I am
thirty-six.

But this Solly Stein, this heavy, green-eyed man
with a thick pink dash on his neck from it looks like
a tracheotomy operation, goes through my résumé
with a silver mechanical pencil. He underlines. He
jots in the margins. In one year, not one Hollywood
producer has studied my résumé like this. A silly old
feeling comes, which I get always for my directors:
I want to make a baby with this Solly Stein.

As he reads and I wait, and all those beautiful
actresses sweat outside, and his assistant pushes
back her cuticles with eraser of her pencil, I confess
to him my Hollywood failure.

"In Soviet Union, all you need is degree from
Leningrad Institute of Theater and to be on right side

of the Party. Acting parts come like airplanes waiting to land."

"It's hard, no doubt about it," he says. "But one
day . . ."

He talks and reads at the same time, something
I cannot do, even in Russian. But I feel as good as
though he awarded me the part. "When I was coming
through Vienna on my way here, I had appointment
with a guy from American Embassy. He gave me
good tips. One, be on time. Two, have initiative. I
think more émigrés do not have this initiative because meaning to them isn't clear. My English is
damn near perfect, but even I have to look it up." I
admit I play a little the role of a fresh-faced immi-
grant, but it amuses him. He laughs. It was deep and
raspy, his laugh, like full garbage cans dragged over
asphalt.

"I see here you did a picture with Elem," he
says.

"You know Elem Yeravansky? He is such a brilliant guy! And young! Did you know he is forty-two
years only?"

"I just met him briefly at Cannes."

"I work with him on film called *Keep Your Guts*.
Is about a woman heavy truck driver, me. Do not
confuse with heavy *woman* truck driver—although
it was necessary to put on some kilos for the role. I
also did my own stunt driving. That title is bad translation. It should be *Keep Your Wits*." I allow a *v* to
slip in instead of *w* on "wits." I know better, but I
am auditioning for a tantalizing émigré, right?

*"Keep Your Vits?"* He laughs very hard, but except his big face, nothing on him moves. His elegant
cream-colored shirt is so starched, so ironed, it holds
him in like a girdle. On table behind where he sits
he has a Styrofoam cup of black coffee and a can of

pink grapefruit juice. He sips first from one, then the other. My mouth shivers at the thought of those tastes together. "Charming," he says. "In fact, perfect. No, wait. I know this." He thinks, running his little finger under the top fold of his ear. "*Ochin khorosho*. Right?"

"Perfect," I say.

"I took two semesters in college," he says.

After my audition I go to meet my friend Claire at Thai Palace in West Los Angeles. She is a girl I know from Slavic Languages Department where I work teaching Russian. When I arrive, I see Thai Palace is demolished. Claire and I ate together there last Wednesday only, but now in its place is a huge hole. At the bottom of the hole sits a yellow tractor machine for lifting dirt.

Just then Claire pulls up. Out passenger window of her car she yells, "Can you believe this? I called last night to see when they opened for lunch, and they told me twelve o'clock." She suggests another restaurant, down the street.

Claire is secretary of Slavic Languages Department, also a screenwriter. She has taken me under her wing about Hollywood. When I first knew her, she was a shy, earnest girl. She dressed all the time in Levi blue jeans. Then she got an affair with our writer in residence, also an émigré. She wrote a screenplay about her and this man, a tender Soviet-American love story, which no one wanted. People loved it, she said, but they did not want it. They said it was beautiful, brilliant, but they would not return her telephone calls. Someone said if she set it in Mexico and added an extraterrestrial, they would certainly want it. It broke her heart to do this, but she

did it, then they lost interest completely. They said
that Russians had been Done.

Hollywood poisoned her system. She suspects
even the menu. "This *says* Australian wild boar. What
d'you want to bet they're just pork chops?" When
our waitress comes, Claire asks about this.

"The boars are raised in Arkansas but slaugh-
tered here. It comes with an Indonesian mint sauce.
I had it yesterday."

"So they aren't really from Australia."

"No, but the breed is."

Claire has an ability to arch one eyebrow only.
This eyebrow is an alarm sensitive to any form of
deception. It leaps up now under her curly reddish-
brown bangs. She orders salad and a banana milk
shake. After our waitress leaves, she says, "They
can't very well be *wild* if they're *raised* in Arkansas,
can they?" She pulls up her foot and sits on it, anxious to hear everything. "Well, is there any reason to
hope?"

"There is always reason to hope."

Chastened a little, she looks down at her fork.
"I mean, what happened? Did he like you? Tell me
from the beginning. You went to the office, and the
secretary handed you a clipboard with a pencil attached by a dirty string. . . ." Her hazel eyes make
happy crescents over her big cheeks. This is a joke
that goes between us. At my first cattle call, many
months ago, she demanded to know all details. I
mentioned the dirty string tying the pencil to the
clipboard. She interpreted this several ways: it was
low-budget production; the role for which I was auditioning was unimportant; the secretary was trying
to find little ways to irritate the casting director, who
was her lover.

"This string was virgin," I say. "I was first one

at the audition. There is place on sign-in sheet where you are supposed to write who is your agent. I wrote, 'No agent, but I was famous actress in Moscow.' "

"You're *kidding*," says Claire. "Either they'll think that's really cute or really stupid. No, fresh— they'll say you're fresh. Or a crackpot. What else?"

I tell her all I can remember. You know those people who can stare at you a long time without blinking? She is one. She says nothing is unimportant in decoding the absurdity of Hollywood.

"How does he look? Last year he was in some big car wreck. His car flipped over twice on Mulholland."

"He has scars on his forehead and neck. He is big guy too, out of shape. You know how people on diets look panicky a little? That was him." I tell about the black coffee and grapefruit juice.

Claire laughs. "Maybe you made him nervous. When is the callback sheet up?"

"He said he will get back to me. He said if it wasn't this, then perhaps something else. He called me perfect."

Both Claire's eyebrows shoot up under her bangs. She is astonished. "He said *that?* He said those *exact* words? How did it go? You finished reading and got ready to leave, and what did he say?"

I repeated it. "Do you think it's real?"

"It sounds real. What reason would he have to get your hopes up?" In silence, we thought. Claire says figuring out reasons why Hollywood people do what they do is like trying to count germs in a public toilet.

A week, then two.

My telephone has power; alive but silent. I cup my palm along the gentle beige curve of the receiver, caressing my future. I try to draw a ring from those thin colored wires inside. One hot evening, I stand outside my apartment building, pretending to enjoy a sooty red sunset. I cock my head to the wires, listening, so I can know what a call sounds like going into my apartment. The sun drops behind the houses across the street. The wires chirr, bip, hum with calls for my neighbors.

My own mind whirs, day and night: he was called out of town, he is busy rewriting, the Fourth of July weekend, he is sick, dead, his assistant lost my telephone number, she transposed the numbers by mistake, she dropped it and it became stuck on sole of her shoe. One day I call to make sure his office is still there, then hang up quick when someone answers.

Claire tells me if he calls and I am not home (when am I not home? I never leave my telephone), he will never call back. "You need an answering machine. If you don't have an answering machine, he'll think you're not serious about being an actress."

I sell some Russian amber I managed to sneak through Immigration, to purchase most expensive model in the store. I somehow believe the more money I spend, the bigger sacrifice I make, the more chance I have of a telephone call. I set up the machine and leave. The longer I stay out of my apartment, the more chance Solly Stein has to call. I drive my Datsun around Beverly Hills, race up and down Sunset Boulevard admiring billboards, go to a movie, the laundromat, eat falafels. When I return at night, the cold red eye of my answering machine stares back at me so cruel. No messages.

"I'm not surprised," says Claire. "When he said he'd call, it really meant you should call him. It meant that at least you wouldn't have to go and hang out with everyone else, waiting in the street for the callback sheet to be posted. You've been promoted to a more privileged level of misery."

Slavic Languages Department holds no summer classes, so Claire is alone to tend our office. I come and eat lunch with her almost every day. Pages of her screenplay are spread all over the floor. There is no air-conditioning in our old humanities building, so Claire looks every day dressed for the beach.

"Okay. If I should call, I call."

"Well, not Monday, because that's the beginning of the week, and not Tuesday, because that's when all the *important* people who didn't call Monday call. Wednesday's not bad, but by then he'll already be behind from Monday and Tuesday. Thursday and Friday are out because that's the end of the week." She arches her eyebrow, a little smug with her logic. "In other words, even though you're supposed to call them, it'll always be a bad time."

"You are as rule-bound as any Soviet," I say.

I pull her telephone across the desk to where I sit. While I dial, she says, "It's lunchtime now. No one'll be in the office until after two-thirty at the earliest. Now's the *worst* time to call." She peels open her sandwich, one of those that appear to be meat but are truly mashed-up beans. I watch her pick out the tomatoes and toss them into garbage can beside her desk.

After many rings, a breathless voice answers. "SollyStein'sofficecanyoupleasehold?" She is gone before I can speak, then she's back. "Thanks for holding."

"Mr. Solly Stein, is he there, please?"

"Who may I say is calling?"

"Tanya Zlopak. I au—"

"One moment, please."

She goes. I perspire all over. My scalp. In between my legs. The receiver is slick in my hand. I smile weakly at Claire. She grins and winks, the mashed bean sandwich poking out her cheek.

"Hiya! How have you been?" This is an unfamiliar voice.

"Excuse me, I wait for Mr. Solly Stein, please."

"Tanya, this is Echo Parchman. I auditioned you with Solly." Ah ha, the assistant.

"Hello, yes. Mr. Stein says he is going to call me, and I was not hearing, so—"

Claire whispers, "Tell them you have another offer and you need to know today." I wave her away.

"Of course!" says Echo Parchman. "This was for . . ."

I am confused. If she remembers auditioning me, doesn't she know what she auditioned me for? "I tried for the role of older but still alluring Russian émigré in his new—"

"Oh, right! Let me see what's happened with that."

I am on hold for some time. Inside the telephone I hear a gentle *tick tick tick*, like a faraway bomb. I stare out the window. A row of palm tree tops rest on the lower ledge. We are on the third floor. They are the strangest trees on earth.

Echo Parchman returns. "Tanya, hiya. Listen, Solly needs to talk to you, but he's tied up right now. When is a good time for him to reach you?"

"Oh, anytime. I have answering machine on my telephone—"

"Does Tuesday the twenty-fourth sound good?"

"July twenty-fourth?" This is three weeks away.

"Terrific. Thanks for checking in, Tanya."

"Uh, thank you."

"Thank *you*."

I hang up. You know the look of people coming off those amusement park rides that go upside down and backwards at eighty miles an hour? That was my look.

Claire reaches over and squeezes my arm. "The thing about this place is that there's always the illusion of things happening when really nothing is happening. Solly Stein's probably sitting in his office right now eating some dietetic gourmet lunch and reading *Variety*. He probably hasn't even *thought* about casting this movie."

Claire was right. He had not thought about it. If he had, he would not have awarded the role of the sensual, worldly Russian émigré, a character whom he described to me at my audition as "an aging beauty born into prerevolutionary-style gentility," to a twenty-three-year-old rock-and-roll singer who has gained her reputation not even singing, but by television commercials for panty hose.

I did not learn I was passed over by receiving a telephone call on Tuesday, July 24. On Tuesday, July 24, I received no telephone call. Not Wednesday, not Thursday either. On Friday I purchased a weekly *Variety* at a newsstand on the corner of Hollywood and Las Palmas. It was on second page, the announcement that this panty hose person wins the role.

I telephoned Solly Stein from Hollywood Boulevard. An anonymous, filthy pay telephone. The receiver was greasy, someone had urinated on the yellow pages. Traffic dragged by. I could hardly hear when I was put through to Echo Parchman. I explain situation. How Solly Stein was going to call me, then didn't, how I read about the role in *Variety*, how he had said there might be something else in the movie if the leading role didn't work out. Echo Parchman said she was surprised he had not called, but he was now on vacation for three weeks. Is it possible he could telephone me in August sometime?

I have never wasted time trying to understand why people do what they do. Is Soviet personality trait. You ask too many questions and you don't get any kind of work, ever, period. I say sure, he can call me whenever. I hang up. I could go right home and lock myself in with the television until I teach again my Russian classes in September, but it would be admitting my immigration was for nothing, that I might have just stayed in Moscow playing forever good-natured Socialist heroines, making love to my vindictive Valentin in my brown-walled apartment.

I force myself back to newspaper stand to buy a *Dramalogue* to see about more cattle calls. The newspaper girl, who has the five-inch fingernails of an old Chinese sage, slips me her copy for free. "You look like you could use some strokes," she says.

From Claire: "He probably *did* really like you. He probably *did* think you were perfect. But this rock singer is hot. She's what they call *bankable.* She's completely wrong for the part, sure, but they'll rewrite. The studio probably wouldn't let him make the movie unless he cast her. That's where the major-league bullshit comes in. If he wants to make his movie, he's got to cast a bubble-brained cretin from a panty hose ad." She has in her eyes that green-eyed gleam. Her wild eyebrows lurch up and down.

We are having dinner at a restaurant on Third Street where Claire says many Hollywood people eat and perform business. I have held off telling her my unhappy news for almost a month, just to avoid her enthusiastic cynicism. The people here are mostly men, suntanned and overworked, in Levi blue jeans and expensive leather shoes. They eat large salads and scribble on yellow pads anchored under their elbows. Claire says all the waitresses are also actresses. She says perhaps it would be better for me to have a job here instead of teaching Russian. She says I need exposure. I need the right kind of people to notice me. I need a shtick. I need, I need.

I concentrate on looping a green noodle over my fork. My neck is tight. "All I need is opportunity to show my talent."

"It'd be great if it were that simple. I read an article about what it takes to make it in Hollywood. They had a list. Number one, connections; number two, perseverance; three was 'being fun to work with'; and four was talent. Can you believe it?"

I don't answer. I make motions to leave.

"Are we done? Don't you want dessert?"

"No. I would like to go."

"What's wrong? I haven't depressed you, have I? I only want you to know how hard it is. A lot of émigrés think that just because this is America, things'll be easy."

"I know it is hard, Claire. But I am unable to hear it anymore, okay?"

We divide the bill and go outside. On western end of street, the sun slides through streaks of purple and red. Claire and I stand on the curb, waiting for a break in traffic so we can cross. I point at the sky. "Is it true that poisons cause this great beauty?"

Claire turns her head west but doesn't really look. "Probably."

"Now *you* are depressed," I say.

She says nothing. In the silence of people who have argument, we watch the cars pass. The light at the end of the block turns red, halting traffic. We are about to walk, but several cars continue through the intersection. The one in the lane closest to us is a beautiful sea-green Rolls-Royce, license plate REEL.

I feel as though someone has dropped an anvil on me. I want to cower, to run back in the restaurant, to wave and stamp feet. "Solly Stein," I cry to Claire.

"What? Where?"

The Rolls slides toward us, close to the curb. Solly Stein does not see us. He pays no attention to driving. He cranes his head to see whose car is in parking lot of this popular Hollywood restaurant. He is also eating something, madly chewing, madly looking, not at all watching the road.

My opportunity. My connection. It will pass in leather-upholstered, air-conditioned oblivion. I have only several seconds to consider my options. Is it a wonder, being an actress of many years, an actress once well known and well loved in Soviet Union, that I opt for most dramatic one?

I lunge into the street. As I hurl myself down on the asphalt, in the silent, endless instant before screeching of brakes and Claire yelling my name and my shoes skidding off, it comes to my mind that I am dealing in Hollywood. This strange powerful person might just run me over, *thump thump, thump thump,* like driving over a dead piece of shag carpet dropped on the freeway.

But I have faith in this stunt, which I performed myself in *Keep Your Wits*, and somehow, crazy crazy, in my director, Solly Stein. The idea is to act hit before you really are. As I fall, the bottom of the license plate slices into the meaty part of my calf. My skirt scrapes up over my thighs. My legs are good, not muscular but shapely. Sensual and world-weary. The

nice legs of a *real* Soviet émigré. I leave the skirt up.
I want him to suffer. Twenty-three-year-old panty
hose queens! Who can believe this world! My eyes
are closed. Heat and wet flow from the leg wound.
Claire squeaks out my name. A car door slams. Frantic footsteps, expensive-soled shoes.

"Oh, God. Christ, no." Solly Stein's voice is torn.
This is perfect. Much better than the actor playing opposite me in *Keep Your Wits*, who ordered me
brusquely to stand up and continue on for the sake
of our Motherland.

Claire kneels next to me, asking about broken
bones, spinal injury, wondering aloud if I can be
moved. Her purse she has slid under my head, the
end of a hairbrush pokes into my scalp. She is so
practical now, in what she thinks is an emergency.
Why not this practicality about Hollywood?

I open my eyes. I don't want Claire to think I'm
in too bad shape. To get a dazed look, I push everything out of focus. Behind her I see the creamy linen
mound that is Solly Stein. He stands with his arms
limp, utterly useless. An ugly dark mass covers his
chest. Blood? How can it be?

Not blood, no. I would feel less bad, less
ashamed, if it were. Then it would be only the inside
of his body paraded out for all to see, instead of the
inside of his mind. It is chocolate, the ghastly smear.
His chubby fingers grasp a king-size candy bar. *Now
47% More!* says one edge of the wrapper. A chocolaty
clot of nuts and caramel hangs from the lapel of his
cream linen jacket.

Some people appear out of the restaurant. They
know Solly Stein. Everyone knows Solly Stein. They
clap his shoulders. What happened? What happened? Tough going, man. A few look down at me

curiously. Is she all right? A little joke goes around, started by a guy I recognize from a popular television series, that the candy bar is the murder weapon. One man slips a card into my hand. He says he's a lawyer.

"A lawyer? Christ." Solly Stein's shoulders heave, his face is weary, tearless but wrecked. "I'm through."

I do not want public humiliation for this man, and certainly not his career to be through. But I have already begun. I have already left Valentin, relinquished my Soviet citizenship, sold my amber. There is nowhere to go. I will persevere. I will be fun to be with.

"Please," I say, "no lawyer. I am all right."

"I'm calling an ambulance," says Claire.

"No, no ambulance," I say, rising on one elbow.

"You need an ambulance," says Solly Stein, not convinced. He moves a few steps toward me.

I take his hand in both of mine and pull him down to me. "Please, I am very poor. I have no moneys. Is embarrassing. I have no insurance for hospital. I be okay."

"Tanya, you have to see a doctor," says Claire. "Look at your leg. You probably need stitches." She stands, wipes her hands, bits of gravel trickling off the heels of her palms. She, of the judgmental dark eyebrow, reader of subtext, expert on Hollywood deception, believes this is an accident. I dare not wink. I dare not whisper, take advantage, mingle with these people, pass to Solly Stein the screenplay I know is stashed in your purse.

"No, I am fine. No ambulance." I wobble a little, hang on Solly Stein's arm as I stand. "My shoes."

One of them was slung into the street, then run

over. Solly Stein, grateful for something to do, scoots to retrieve it. He tries to push it back into shape, buffs it on his sleeve.

"We can go to my doctor. He'll take care of the leg," says Solly Stein.

Claire folds her arms. "She should go to the hospital."

"I am all right. This will work." I try to make my eyes communicate to her my trick.

"Please, what did you say your name was? Tawny?"

Solly Stein does not remember. Is just as well. Then I am not the eager émigré he would not call back. I am a new actress. The one who was helpless and foreign, who would not sue him, who gently took the candy bar from his fat paw and threw it into the gutter, who rode away with him in his Rolls-Royce, straight into the shameless Los Angeles sunset.

"Tanya," I say. "Tanya Zlopak."

There is another fact of Hollywood I will use this day to my advantage: in Los Angles, to drive anywhere is forty-five minutes. Forty-five minutes I have now to speak to Solly Stein. Not of my brilliance, but of his. To speak, actress to director, of his technique, his sensitivity, his ability to extract the most impossible performances. To summon into his sea-green eyes that look I often confuse with love. That look which says, Let us make something together.

# LENIN LIVES

## JIM SPANIEL

There, in the small, warm tomb, ripe with the smell of damp wool and many not unpleasant body odors, shoulder to shoulder with several dozen Soviets, some of whom are openly weeping, I gaze down at the tidy waxen face of Vladimir Ilyich Lenin and am reminded of Lidia. Not to suggest that Lidia Nikolaevna looks embalmed. Or that Lenin looks like a sassy, small-waisted modern-day Soviet black marketeer. The point is this: in the same way the song playing during your first kiss gets mated with that memory forever—even if, as in my case, it was a jingle for water beds—V. I. Lenin, calm and dead and stared at daily, will always remind me of my wife. My estranged wife, I should say.

The last time I saw Lenin was with Lidia on our wedding day. I insisted on a typical Soviet wedding, with all the trimmings: the major one being a visit to the tomb after our ceremony at the Palace of Marriage. Lidia looked gorgeous, in an expensive lacy wedding dress that I had brought with me from Los Angeles. I had purchased the gown according to her specifications, but it was still a size too small. That night I ran my tongue all around her, over the soft red marks left by the seams.

I've seen Lenin eleven, now twelve times. I bring a group of my college students to Moscow every summer, and the mausoleum is one of our first stops. Lenin was a small man; in one of my recent articles, I've drawn comparisons between him and Napoleon, as well as other teeny despots in history. I'm up for tenure next year, and even though I'm good with my students, my publishing record is weak. I'm here now, during semester break, to whip up a quick monograph on, for example, budding consumerism in contemporary Soviet society.

There is also the question of whether I should see Lidia, who returned to Moscow after living with me in California for less than six months.

Her leaving crushed me. I moped and drank. I licked my wounds by imagining her shell-pink neck under the wheels of a tank rolling through Red Square on May Day; by envisioning her lovely, powerful hands engaged in hard labor in some frozen place far away from the pretty clothes she lived for.

One bad night, I found a pair of panties she'd left behind flattened at the bottom of the laundry hamper and slept with them laid out on her empty pillow. This was finally the last humiliating straw. I pulled myself together. Thoughts of suicide were replaced with bodybuilding and a general course of self-improvement. I organized volleyball games between the various humanities departments, had a few dates with an assistant professor from the Department of Spanish and Portuguese.

I wrote an article on the psychological implications of the breakup of the cross-cultural marriage, consoling myself with the thought that I was beefing up my curriculum vitae.

There are several hours a week when Lenin's mausoleum is open only to foreign tourists and the line is short. This, of course, compromises the viewing experience. It's not the same as waiting in line for three hours with regular Russians, who are chided by the spiffy, uniformed KGB officers patrolling the line not to talk, not to slouch, not to stand with arms folded or hands in pockets. Personally, I'd rather wait with the Russians.

"You are demented!" Lidia had said when I told her this. "Why choose to suffer?"

"What's the point of seeing Lenin's tomb with tourists? You have to see Lenin with Russians. Lenin doesn't mean anything to East Germans or Indians. He's a freak show."

"What do you think he is to Russians?" Lidia Nikolaevna is among those who believe that Lenin is not really Lenin, that he's the creation of an expert candlemaker. "Nobody who was dead sixty-five years looks like that. People are bones by then."

"They say he gets refurbished every year."

"Those are lies. If you were Russian, you would understand this."

This conversation took place on the day Lidia and I met, last July. I had sixteen college juniors with me and was merely passing a gift on to her from a friend. The gift-giving evolved into bottle-sharing: expensive French wine which Lidia had traded for some beat-up Earth Shoes she had procured from a wandering hippie. She called them Shoes of the Earth, which lent them and her black-market dealings a sort of biblical quality. I was captivated. She had straight light-yellow hair and pale Slavic features, startling cheekbones you could set a glass on. She looked like the drawing of Lara in the copy of *Doctor Zhivago* I had read in sixth grade.

We were sitting knee to knee at the small wooden table in her apartment. I had left my students back at the hotel, resting up from a day at the Exhibition of Economic Achievement. I was hoping, but not daring to hope . . . I had never been with a pure Russian woman. The closest I had come was a girl in graduate school who had a mother from Minsk and a father from Pagan, Nebraska. Lidia Nikolaevna would be interesting and beneficial, both physically and intellectually. Perhaps something could be developed on Marxism-Leninism as it impacts the Soviet woman's sexuality. There were all sorts of possibilities.

But Lidia was not without her own agenda. She counted questions off on her big-knuckled fingers: Who is the most famous person you know? Do you know any movie stars? Have you ever been shot at?

The most famous person I know is Sergei Lublinsky, who works in our department. I thought it would impress her that I knew Russian émigré literature. I expounded for a few minutes on how Lublinsky's work compared to that of other writers of his generation, both Soviet and émigré. She was politely disinterested. "What movie stars?" she asked.

I said I once saw Charlton Heston buying Cool Whip at the grocery store near my apartment.

"You shop together in *same* store?"

"Not together. I see him occasionally. I saw him that once, anyway."

"Who else?" She leaned forward, pulling a strand of hair across her lips. "You make me fascinated."

Let me say in my own defense that it is not often that women find me or what I have to say fascinating. I am a man women turn to when they need help with men. One woman friend once said, "Jim, it's so great being with you. There's absolutely no sexual tension between us."

So my telling Lidia Nikolaevna, there in her cherished though unkempt apartment, with the exotic, cantaloupe-colored light of the Russian summer night sun filtering through the window, and Lidia leaning toward me, touching her lips, lowering her eyes, going through all number of seductive motions, which, I deduced much later, she picked up from American women's magazines, that Clint and I were like that, that Warren and I did weights together at my health club, that Dustin is practically a regular around the Department of Slavic Languages and Literatures, is forgivable. Understandable anyway. Especially since I doubted she knew who these people were. I told her, between kisses, that I had been shot at six times. On the Universal Studios tour, which I did not tell her.

With bayonets poised, the guards hurry you in, around the coffin, and out, for which I'm grateful. I'm anxious to record my response at seeing Lenin again. I kneel down right there on the frozen stones of Red Square, balance my notebook on my knee, wag my pen to get it going. *Like Proust w/fateful madeleine. Seeing V. I. and I ache for Lidia. It all comes back. Possible article? How V. I. Lenin Helped Reunite Young Prof with Soviet Wife. Too tabloid. Another angle? Will Lidia even see me?*

Whenever I'm in Moscow alone, I'm followed by some bored, barrel-shaped man in a navy-blue overcoat and fedora. I'm of interest for no particular reason, other than that I travel to the Soviet Union more than the average American and speak Russian. The barrel they've got attached to me this trip bears a startling resemblance to an ex-President, and yesterday, while we stood together at the crowded champagne bar in the G.U.M. department store, pretending we didn't know each other, I turned to him and said, "Has anyone ever told you that you look like a Slavic version of Ronald Reagan?"

Without acknowledging me, he guzzled the rest of his champagne, stood up, wandered out. I had a strange feeling maybe I only imagined I had spoken to him.

I expect him to crop up now as I walk back to my hotel, but he's nowhere to be seen.

The style of my hotel is Twentieth-Century Gargantuan: fifty stories of glass and reinforced concrete, with the same beauty and seductive charm of the gray-cinder-block-and-board bookcases found in the apartments of my students. I am on the twenty-third floor, in room 2356. Outside, in front, a crew of wide-hipped old women with flowered babushkas knotted under their chins push black slush into piles along the gutter. I stand and watch them for a moment, trying to think how I should approach Lidia. I hadn't written to tell her I was coming, in case I didn't have the courage to face her once I was here. I could go to her right now, or I could go to my room and write. I could go get something to eat first. I could forget the whole thing.

Just as I'm about to go inside, I'm stopped by a youngish man with a face as pink as boiled shrimp. His hand is closed tight against his thigh.

Slowly, it opens, like the crusty shell of a sea crea-
ture. I peek inside. Cradled in his palm are what appear to be war medals. "For this," he says. He
thumps my chest. His eyes are large and black and
nearly lashless. He reminds me of a yard pest, a
mole, gopher, or groundhog, that in theory should be
cute and harmless but is somehow too sinister.

"This?" I answer in Russian, plucking at the
front of my shirt. I'm dressed Soviet style in a white
dress shirt, thick-soled black shoes, shapeless overcoat, and fur hat, in order to discourage just this
kind of thing. I'm interested in studying the Soviet
black market, not in participating in it.

"No. Hard Rock Café," he sputters in English.
I'm surprised. Notwithstanding *glasnost*, it is still
uncommon for a Soviet to speak English to a foreigner in public. I'm also impressed with his eyesight. Under my white dress shirt I have on a T-shirt
for extra warmth. I look down to see crimson writing
bleeding through the white cotton: HARD ROCK CAFÉ,
LOS ANGELES.

"Vadim sees." He smiles. "Vadim knows." His
teeth are studded with tiny, whiskey-colored cavi-
ties.

I lift one of the medals from his hand. They are
made out of a stiff gold plastic, like something you
might find in a box of cereal. How stupid did this
Vadim think I was? "What are these?"

His gaze drops to a point in space just under my
left earlobe. He rolls his lips inside his mouth. "Medals. World War Two."

"These aren't medals. And if they were, I could
get arrested taking them out of the country."

He shrugs and takes a small vial out of his
pocket. Peppermint oil, which he applies to his teeth
with his finger. The oil is potent, and in the freezing

cold the smell of it scours out my entire nasal cavity.
I dig my nose inside my collar and get a faint whiff
of Lidia's perfume, which still lingers in the fabric
of the T-shirt.

"Icons, then. You like icons?"

The conversation is pointless. I have no inten-
tion of trading this T-shirt.

It was a birthday present from Lidia. I wear it
even though I am opposed, in principle, to clothing
with any form of writing on it. She will tell you that
I only arrived at this principle *after* I learned she had
stolen the T-shirt from the display case at the restaurant, while the hostess was seating other customers.
This is not true. Yes, I was unhappy that she had
begun shoplifting; yes, I wasn't wild about her
scheme of buying clothes on sale at one store and
returning them at another store for full price; yes, I
grew impatient with her insistence on trying to bar-
gain, barter, haggle with, and underbid the checkers
at the West Hollywood Alpha Beta, but I would never
pretend to believe in something I didn't in order to
communicate my anger. I would be silent and, according to Lidia, surly.

Except for the last one, our arguments were
embarrassingly the same. They would begin by my
telling Lidia, again, that her black-market antics
would have to end, or by Lidia complaining of a
headache, caused, she said, by heat or boredom or
sensory overload (a term she picked up from me).
Sometimes I heard: "People in America don't spend
enough time with their wives," or: "People in America are stingy." "People in America are too studious"
was my favorite. The whole country got blamed for
the reason she was mad at me. Then I got blamed
for not understanding her because I wasn't Russian, which deteriorated into getting blamed for not

being Russian. Los Angeles got accused of not being Moscow.

"Then why are you here?" I shouted.

She didn't know. She must have been demented to marry me. Where were all the movie stars, anyway? She blew her nose into a blouse that still had the tags dangling from one sleeve.

"Maybe you should go home," I whispered.

"You don't dispose me so easy," she snapped.

I gave up. I got quiet.

I began to take notes for a book on the everyday psychodynamics of the Soviet émigré experience.

I manage to convince this Vadim person that I have nothing to sell him—no *disks*, no *valkmans*, no Levi *dzhinsy*, but he lingers around the front of the hotel, occasionally glancing over in my direction. I decide it's probably better not to go up to my room, even though I'm sure he's harmless.

There is a liquor store on Gorky Street, where Russians buy wine according to the alcohol content. I go there and ask for something at twenty percent that's not too sweet. My plan is this: return to my room and drink my wine, then go to Kalinin Prospekt and throw myself at Lidia's feet. The wine is to ensure that I do this with American savvy and good taste.

On the floor of every hotel in the Soviet Union is an elderly woman who sits there all day, on guard. Intourist will tell you she's there to make sure that all your needs are attended to, that no one bothers you. She's really there to keep her fellow citizens out. My guard is elderly and overweight and partial to the color orange (orange dress, orange shoes). On my return, she is dozing, her head on her chest. She looks like a collapsed pumpkin. She starts when I walk past. I make no effort to tiptoe, which looks sneaky. Her tiny blue eyes run over me, then rest accusingly on the wine bottle.

"Courage," I say, holding it up and winking.

"Stupidity," she snorts.

At four o'clock it's already dark, and the air is thick and cottony, promising snow. I can feel the expression of determination freeze on my face as I set out to find my wife.

Most foreigners regularly send home a postcard of Kalinin Prospekt, the one that shows a row of four huge glass office buildings at night, their windows lit up to spell CCCP. The secretary in the Slavic Department has this postcard up on her bulletin board, over her desk. I used to stare at it when no one else was around, thinking perhaps I'd locate three or four dots of color which represented Lidia and her yellow-flowered canvas suitcase, from which she sells her Western shoes and clothing.

It is this suitcase I see now, grazing the wool and polyester legs of pedestrians as Lidia strolls down the sidewalk in the middle of rush hour. A single hot-pink high heel juts from between the teeth of the zipper; the one prick of color in this brown-and-gray place. I'm suddenly struck with nostalgia for my wife's perpetual state of disarray. The cigarette butts and piles of ash she'd leave on the arm of the sofa. The arcs of dirt on the bathroom towels, evidence of a rare and possibly divine inspiration to dust the furniture.

I stand in front of the Institut Krasoti Beauty Salon, watching Lidia walk away from me. A woman exits the salon, releasing a host of stinging beauty parlor smells. She stares at me, wondering about the tears leaking down my face. I tell her it's the burning hair. Too close to the dryer. She looks nonplussed. Russians never need an excuse to cry.

I'm not sure people behaved this way before the movies revolutionized our ideas on love and reconciliation (certainly worth looking into: The Media as They Impact the Soviet-American Romance?), but the closer I get to Lidia, the more urgent it becomes to see her. I push past old men with dusty war medals, real ones, rusted to their coats. I elbow my way through troops of young women with closed, tired faces, scuttling home in their poorly made shoes. After all this time, after months of refusing to accept Lidia's long-distance phone calls, refusing to answer her letters, refusing to think about her, but thinking about her constantly; after days of trudging around Moscow observing the behavior of women standing in line for Yugoslavian shower curtains, studying the way teenagers caress the pins and buttons that decorate their jackets, noting the precious care car owners take with their windshield wipers (removing them at night so they won't get stolen), but avoiding this street, her phone number, the way to her apartment, I am desperate. I am in love.

"Lidia Nikolaevna."

She turns. I notice, happily and immediately, that her hair has returned to its former straight yellow state. The first thing she had done in Los Angeles was to give herself a crunchy home permanent.

"Jim! Oi—what is this—when—I cannot believe—how you are?" She puts her suitcase down but doesn't reach up to hug me, as I expected. She rubs her arms, to give her hands something to do. "You should tell me when you come."

"Didn't you get my letter?"

"When did you mail it?"

"I can't remember. Three weeks ago maybe."
Why didn't I write, call? Guilt forces me to stare at
the toes of her shoes.

"Hm. I'll have to check next door. The man there
is named Boris Nikolavich, and I am Lidia Nikolaevna Borisova. There are all kinds of things." She
shakes her head, looking past me. All her problems
are addressed in this small gesture, and suddenly I
feel as if I've missed a lot.

"More than just not getting your mail?"

"Kolya is in hospital." She taps the side of her
head. "You know, for rehabilitation. The dummy
signed some petition involving Sakharov or something." Kolya is Lidia's brother. On our honeymoon,
she told me that he is as obsessed with America as I
am with the Soviet Union. Even though I've only met
him twice, I'm very fond of him.

"My God, Lidia, when? That's terrible."

"Don't get on your face that look—'Oh, the poor
Soviet people, they are so mistreated.' He should
have his head checked for doing that here. Was not
wise." Her surprise has settled into irritation. She
stamps her feet. "California has killed my blood cells.
I've been cold all winter."

I smile, grateful for any reference to the past.
"You look great."

"I need some good face cream. You do not bring
any, do you?"

"I brought some cinnamon-flavored dental
floss."

"For crow's-feet?"

I laugh stupidly. "I guess not."

"Well, where is it? You have it here?"

"It's back at the hotel. Listen, can't we go back
to your place and talk?"

"It's bad I have marriage to a foreigner on my

record, Jim. You know." She nods down at her live-lihood, the canvas suitcase and every illegal thing inside it. "Why are you here, anyway?"

"I'm—well, I came to see you. I'm also writing some articles, you know—"

"Articles? Articles such as—what is that title? Oh. How can one forget? Is so brilliant. 'Lara in Lo-tusland: A Study of Contemporary Soviet Female Mentality.' "

"Lidichka, please." I begin to sweat, then shake, inside my heavy coat.

" 'Socialism and the Self'? 'The Marketplace versus Marxism'? You take notes right now, right? 'Hysteria in a Closed Society: American Shitheads and Their Soviet Wives.' "

"Lidia, come on, do I look like I'm taking notes?"

"In your head you are!" Tears wobble in her eyes.

"I left my notebook back at my hotel. Please, let's go."

"You go, Jim. Go work on your article." She picks up her suitcase and walks off. The crowd swal-lows her instantly.

I stare after her. I wonder whether she's really still angry at me, or it's that finally, in the end, we got a glimpse of something fierce and pathetic in each other, that tiny pocket of unhinged howling, which Americans fear because they don't realize it's a part of everyone, and Russians fear because they do.

We had not argued for several weeks, simply be-cause I could not be goaded into an argument. My book was coming along. I thought about the house we'd buy after I got tenure. Everything Lidia did was fascinating and useful. *L. walks around the apart-ment while she brushes her teeth. L. uses the "if . . . so" construction when speaking English—yesterday*

*she said, "If you are done with your work today, so
we can go shopping tonight." When asked why she
was depressed, L. said, "It's the ozone." L. refuses to
see other émigrés, claims they're too backward. She
perspires heavily in her sleep. Her skin still smells
foreign, salty—pickled beets?*

One day, while I was at the library, she found
my notes. When I got home, she was sitting on the
edge of the sofa tearing out the pages of my spiral
notebook by the handful. Everything on her wide,
angular face was melting. Mascara dribbled down
her cheeks. Her nose ran. Pockets of spit formed in
the corners of her mouth from hurling all those wet
Russian expletives into the empty apartment.

I was guilty and terrified. I knew instantly what
had happened. She threatened to kill me; I begged
her to. She wadded my notes up with both fists and
pushed the ball into my face, raking my cheeks with
the pointy edges of the paper. Pickled beets! Pickled
beets! she screamed. I said, Yes, yes, I deserved this.
I encouraged it. Kill me, hit me. She stopped. She
wasn't going to give me the satisfaction of penance.
She was leaving. Incredibly, I barred the door, my
body poised in sort of a mid-jumping-jack position.
No, no, she would stay, I would go. I'm leaving. *No,
I'm leaving.* We're both yelling and sobbing. The
neighbor downstairs bangs on his ceiling and hol-
lers, *Why don't you both get the hell out of here?*
Lidia is going, leaving me, stuffing all number of useless things into a grocery bag—panty hose that were
soaking in the kitchen sink, magazines, toothpaste, a
six-pack of diet soda. The instant I lower my arms to
catch her, she flings the door open, squashing me
between it and the wall.

Before she left for Moscow, several weeks later,
she robbed me of everything she had given me, plus

everything she could get a good price for back home. She left me a note saying I was worse than any despicable KGB and dead in bed to boot.

Near my hotel there is a line of shoppers dribbling out the door of a shop that looks as if it has nothing to sell. Their white string bags dangle like empty fishing nets around their knees. Most of them are reading while they wait, dog-eared, much-handled paperbacks printed on inferior Soviet paper that is rumored to give you eczema. Lidia never read, never showed the least interest in my work. I feel righteous, lucky to be rid of her . . . for the exact length of time it takes me to articulate the thought.

Up on the twenty-third floor, the woman who guards the corridor is not at her post. As I round the corner, I see her coming from the direction of my room, jingling a ring of keys. Walking a few paces behind her, head down, is Vadim of the cereal box war medals. This is extraordinary. A corridor lady not at her post. A Russian strolling the halls of an off-limit tourist hotel. But I'm too despondent to pay much attention. I've got a headache from the Crimean wine I drank earlier and am trying to replace thoughts of Lidia with thoughts about my socks. My toes are numb from the walk back. My socks are either too thin, in which case I'm getting frostbite for obvious reasons, or too thick, binding my feet, inhibiting the circulation. I've been to Moscow several times in the winter and can never get this worked out. I lift up my foot and jiggle my toes around.

Vadim doesn't look up as he passes, so I happen, quite accidentally, to catch sight of something even more astounding than his presence: he is bald at the crown of his head and has painted his scalp with what looks like brown shoe polish to approximate

the color of his hair. I'm stunned, excited. A new dis-
covery. Russian men are afraid of balding too!

As I unlock my door, my mind is ablaze: how is
this fear of balding reinforced? No advertising, no
media here. Though in state-approved literature the
perfect Socialist hero always has a full head of hair.
But what about the Politburo? Shiny domes abound.
Fear of balding as a class issue in an allegedly class-
less society?

I really think I'm onto something, when I realize
that my room has been searched.

They are experts. Things appear untouched.
Books and Rolaids on the dresser, running shoes at
the side of the bed, one on its side, lace just so. But
there is the impression of someone's backside on the
bedspread, and the dust on the books has been
mussed. The KGB, yes, of course. But who? My
barrel-bodied shadow, who, until yesterday, was my
constant companion? More likely Vadim. The room
smells slightly of peppermint oil. And the corridor
lady? Naturally, she let him in. And what is her re-
ward for this? Tickets to a hockey game? A special
hairdo at the Institut Krasoti? I fall onto the bed,
careful not to touch the seat print. Why? In case the
police come? They *are* the police. I am overwhelmed
with self-pity; American reflexes are useless in the
real world. I feel like the trite duped foreigner in an
ill-researched spy novel, where everyone who's not
American has the same bad accent and no one speaks
his native tongue in private.

I remember my notebook. I hesitate to glance on
the window ledge where I left it, afraid it's gone.

But it's not. It's been handled, obviously, read
through, probably, laughed at, maybe. Duly noted.
I'm disappointed somehow. If it had been taken, I

could blame the Soviet Union if I didn't get tenure.
Or I could thank it for saving me from myself and
my cockamamy ideas. I could get brooding and
mournful; I could say salvation came too late. Had
my room been visited before I met Lidia, I could have
said to her, honestly, that I'd sworn off note taking,
that I hadn't a notebook to my name. But the notebook is here.

Eagerly, with a twinge of shame, I start making
notes on vanity and the Soviet male.

The phone rings. I presume it's just the KGB,
making sure I'm in.

"If you want to come over, come now. Don't ring
the buzzer. The door will be open." It's Lidia.

"Yes—all right."

Her voice hangs on the other end, silent and re-
proachful. "This is dangerous for me. I had to call a
few hotels to find you." She hangs up.

Lidia lives in a pink brick building on the south-
western edge of the city. A banner stretched across
the entrance says: LENIN LIVED, LENIN LIVES, LENIN WILL
LIVE.

I enter her apartment without knocking, afraid
it might alert the neighbors who get her mail. She is
sitting at her wooden table—the ubiquitous wooden
table, which is part of every Russian household—
bent over a notebook. She stares hard at the page,
her pencil sharpened to a cruel point.

"Is the saying 'to fight fire *with* fire'?"

"What?"

"The American saying. To fight fire with fire. Yes
or no."

I should stop this now. I should be reasonable,
refuse to escalate. I should lean over her, rest my
chin on the top of her cold blond head, smooth my

hands over her shoulders and down her arms, close the notebook, sail it out the window, draw her to me, promise things.

"Yes," I say, trembling, filled with love and dread.

# NOTES FROM A WEDDING SHOWER

## MARINA McINTYRE

I am *not* a KGB agent. I want this understood immediately. Last week a catalogue came to Department of Slavic Languages addressed to Purchasing Agent, but the "Purchasing" had been smeared away and the address just said "Agent." My co-workers put it in my mailbox for a joke. Ha ha! I was furious. I felt like writing a memo: Just because someone is KGB does not mean they are KGB agent. If someone works for the army, are they automatically the one pushing the button? No!

I *inform* for KGB, but I am no agent. Still, I do feel guilty. I eavesdrop on my co-workers' conversations and report them to my handler, Chad. Chad has worked Los Angeles for five years and has gone from Vladimir Stepanovich to Vladimir to Vlad, now Chad. He loves California. He has a recipe for borscht that includes wheat germ and millet.

Did I say I felt guilty? Guilty is not it. My co-workers' conversations are generally tedious. Should I or should I not purchase that sofa love seat on sale? Who is your gynecologist? I do not feel guilty for overhearing these kinds of things.

Chad and I recruit people. For the person who needs quick money and has access to interesting documents, we have a job. We do not get people sent to gulag. Still, I do work for the people who send people to gulag. But I also buy irons made by people who make bombs, so what is that? Did I say I felt guilty? No. Guilt is a classic feeling, an elegant feeling; a glorious crystal cathedral. I should be so deep. What I feel is more base, more pathetic. Picture a tawdry shrine to a second-rate Russian Orthodox saint in the room of some sniveling Dostoevskian hero, and you have an idea how noble my feelings are. More simply, I feel left out.

To give an example of my situation in regard to my co-workers. I share an office with three other Soviet émigrés. The office is windowless, with tall white walls. A plant in an orange plastic pot sits on top of the departmental refrigerator. It is a variety of cactus that is supposed to withstand anything.

They are nice women, Bella, Tanya, and Valeria, the women with whom I share the office, but normally I would never choose them for friends. However, since they all despise me, all I want is their friendship. I am always alone in the office. They say they stay away because I smoke. However, they all smoke too. They are the kind of dim-witted souls who can't think of a decent excuse.

One day after teaching my Elementary Russian II class, I returned to find someone there. I was shocked. It was Bella Semyonovna, the most skittish,

Marina-Pavlovna-hating émigré of all. A snarl of royal-blue ribbon covered her desk.

I said, "Bellichka, what you are doing?" I could *see* what she was doing. Knotted blue mounds sat in a pile at her elbow: she was practicing making bows. At semester's end, Bella was leaving our humble Department of Slavic Languages, the tiniest language department in the university, for a gift-wrapping position at a downtown department store.

Asking what are you doing is a safe question, right? If you were a hand-wringing, paranoid Soviet you wouldn't be intimidated, would you? It is not a dangerous question. It is not, for example: Do you know any jokes about Lenin's sex life?

She said, "Nothing." *Nothing.* She could not say to me, Marina Pavlovna, I practice making bows? Her fists clenched up in the pile of ribbon, white eggs in a blue nest. Did I say I was shocked when I saw her there? Not shocked, *expectant.* Shocked is a cousin of cynicism and resignation. I was expectant. A tiny sparrow of hope flew from my stomach to my throat. I was hoping we could have a conversation, a chat. A trip to student union for a coffee, even. But here was Bella Semyonovna, terrified. I could practically see her palms sweat.

But then she is right. You never know. I might run to the nearest pay phone to report to Kremlin. Each of her bows had a few oversized loops bent at fierce angles. What would I say? Comrade! Bella Semyonovna's bows look like propellers found on World War II bomber planes! Better recruit her or arrest her now, or every grad, dad, and newlywed who receives a gift from Bullock's Downtown will be privy to ancient secrets of Soviet aviation!

But I cannot blame her. I *am* KGB. I *will* talk to

Chad this evening, as I do almost every evening. I don't blame her for giving me a bright panicked smile. For seeing the plant on top of the refrigerator and getting an excuse from it and saying, "Oh! This plant needs water!" and scurrying out of the office, without the plant, without the plastic pitcher we always use for watering, without looking at me.

No, I don't blame her. I blame me.

Before I agreed to inform, Chad made being KGB seem like a branch of foreign service. He took me to lunch at a Venice Beach restaurant where there were no prices on the menu and the waiters wore cotton pants rolled up, portraying their sexy suntanned calves. He didn't tell me that that would be the last time anyone would ever invite me to lunch.


While the people in the Department of Slavic Languages have an idea that I am KGB, my husband, Ted, does not. Because he thinks vodka and *Crime and Punishment* are wonderful and perfect, he thinks Russians must be wonderful or, well, at least not as monstrous as everyone thinks. My adorable American Ted says things like: "I mean, how do we *know* Afghanistan didn't invite them in?"

He thinks Chad is my cousin. This is because I told him Chad was my cousin. Ted believes me. As he should. He is honest with me, and he expects me to be honest with him. But I don't respect him for believing me. I want him to say: "Marina! I can see it in your eyes! You are lying to me! This is no cousin! This Chad is KGB and you are KGB!"

Then I can act insulted, get defensive, break down and weep, throw myself at his feet, beg for mercy, and suggest we start all over again by celebrating at our favorite Vietnamese restaurant, on Olympic Boulevard.

Now, however, whenever Ted answers the telephone I am forced to go into the bathroom and throw my knee-high nylons into the sink. I run the water loud, slosh around the hose, reach over and flush the toilet with my toes. I cannot bear to hear his big, friendly side of the conversation. The more friendly Ted is to Chad, the stupider he seems! He asks Chad, Has the weather been hot enough for you? How about those Dodgers? He talks slow and loud. I want to strangle him.

Then I feel guilty. For wanting to strangle the man I love, for keeping this rather giant secret from him. Honey, I have something to tell you: I dented the car at the supermarket today; also, I am KGB. Did I say guilt? I wish it were guilt. What I actually feel is just a little bad. The way you feel when you start out discussing one friend with another friend and you end up gossiping. Creepy is what I really feel. Creepy, a diluted, Westernized version of guilt, is the best I can do.

The other Soviet émigrés in the department suspect I'm KGB because they suspect everyone is KGB. They might even suspect each other, for all I know. But I know *they* are not KGB, because *I* am KGB.

Claire, secretary to the department, thinks it is all a bunch of bull. Those are her words. A bunch of bull. I overheard her talking on the telephone to a friend. "I don't believe there are any real KGB agents anymore. They're like the secretaries on Capitol Hill—they've all turned into KGB agents-slash-models."

Claire is the type who needs subterfuge, trench coats, microphones masquerading as ballpoint pens, beauty marks, and forged documents. In short, romance. She doesn't realize—nobody realizes—that it's less interesting than bookkeeping and about six times as lonely. Yes, lonely. Sitting in the end stall of the ladies' room listening, sitting in your tiny claustrophobic office listening. Listening, watching. Raging, bitter loneliness is your lot. And self-pity now, see? If there is one thing worse than a KGB informer, it's a self-pitying KGB informer. Well, I am one thing worse.

Because Claire thinks I'm just Marina Pavlovna, teaching assistant for Elementary Russian II and wife of Ted McIntyre, she doesn't shun me. Of course, since she doesn't shun me, her friendship isn't important to me, even though she is someone I like. But even if I did want her friendship, I wouldn't want to get close to her, because then it would be like with Ted. I'd feel creepy for keeping a secret, etc. So I'm civil but aloof.

One day, she came into the office with a tall, fat girl around thirty-five. This girl was Donna Pendell, Valeria's future sister-in-law. Valeria Chalisian, a very sweet, doltish émigré, with heavy Armenian features and an almost pathological inability to dress for Southern Californian weather (she switches to lightweight wool for a heat wave), has left Pyotr, the Russian husband with whom she emigrated, and is going to marry an American, Doug, the brother of this Donna Pendell.

Claire said, "Donna wants to put together a wedding shower for Valeria."

"Not a wedding shower," said Donna, "more of a party. In honor of the wedding. Just a buffet. No decorations. None of those stupid games like you know how they count the number of ribbons the

bride breaks when she opens her gifts and then say
that's the number of children she'll have."

"What?" I just barely got the sense of what a
shower was, now ribbons, now Valeria's children?

"What about the one where the bride traces her
hand over and over again on a paper plate? Do you
know that one?" said Claire.

"No, nothing like that," said Donna.

"What?" I said.

Claire puts her hand flat on my desk and draws
around it with an imaginary pen. " 'Oh, this feels so
funny! Why are you making me do this! This is really
ridiculous!' One person writes down what she says
and then reads it back to her. It's supposed to be
what the bride'll say on her wedding night."

"I want this to be elegant," said Donna.

Donna had bracelets up to her elbows, and the
palest skin, pale as the inside of your arm. "You have
beautiful skin," I said. "You must live under-
ground."

Donna laughed. It boomed off the walls.

Claire said, "Donna wanted to know who could
help her with the shower. She wanted someone who
had, you know, good taste."

"I want something really elegant," said Donna.
"Claire said you used to live in Paris."

"I said you had *been* there," said Claire.

It turned out what Donna wanted was one of
Valeria's friends to help her organize this wedding
shower. She said she wanted it to be a real Soviet-
American venture. I was delighted! I said, sure, yes,
when do we start, what do you need me to do? She
said she'd get back to me. I said, terrific, let's have
it at my apartment. I did not say, "Oh, by the way,
Valeria loathes me," which made me feel slightly de-

ceitful. But, to quote Ted when he is going to spend money we don't have, "What the hell." I was going to give a wedding shower, whatever that was.

There are certain stores around Los Angeles that have wedding shower items, including some silver cardboard bells for hanging up. That very day I went and bought some of these bells and some crepe paper and balloons, but Donna informed me these were tacky and middle-class. We were going to be elegant. We were going to invite men as well as women, she said, and have food that matched the wrapping paper on the gifts.

I told this to Chad one night, and he thought I was crazy.

"Donna is a thing called an image consultant," I said. I knelt by the bed, flipping through recipe books. In the other room I could hear Ted swear at an ice cube tray while banging it against the kitchen counter. "She helps people decide how to represent themselves in society, how to wear their hair, what name to have. Perhaps she has some good clients I could find out about. She said no decorations, but I finally convinced her on my wedding bells, silver foil on cardboard. I got her by saying they are traditional, and traditional is elegant these days."

"What about Valeria's fiancé?" said Chad. He was getting a little impatient with wedding shower talk, I could tell.

"Doug is his name. He works at post office and writes sestinas."

"Sestinas?"

"Poems. He is poet. He cleans floors at post office. I thought maybe he has access to mail, but no."

"A poet in Los Angeles?"

"It's true. He took Valeria's class so he could read our poets in original Russian. That's how they met. Donna wants both Russian and American dishes, to symbolize cross-cultural union. What is, in your opinion, a classic Russian dish?"

"A classic Russian dish?" he asked slowly. "What is wrong with you?"

"Oh, yes! And it has to be orange or purple. This is what makes a problem. Other foods we are having are something with eggplants, then plums, caviar, of course, salmon, and a blackberry-carrot dessert. Beets probably qualify as purple, but borscht is so heavy for this time of year. . . . Chad, are you still there?" He had hung up.

I felt bad that I had upset Chad, but not bad enough to call him back. This was an American wedding shower, and if he was going to be a humorless Russian oaf about it, let him.

I closed my recipe book and went to the nightstand, where I kept my legal papers, my Soviet passport. The longer I am in Los Angeles, the queerer these look. The dingy cheap paper, the faded official stamps. Keeping the papers was part of our deal. I would be KGB if I could keep my Soviet citizenship.

Why did I want to keep my Soviet citizenship if I was going to settle in Los Angeles with my adorable American Ted? One reason. One petty-minded, small-souled reason. I did not want to be an émigré. As long as I knew I could go back, I would not be one of those disoriented, eternally perspiring people stumbling around in the California sunshine. The foreign people with the ugly shoes. But I still want them all to like me! That is the despicable part! Chad, Valeria, Tanya, Bella, the rest of the Russian population here in Los Angeles, as well as back in U.S.S.R.

Everyone, everywhere. Descartes as reinterpreted by Marina Pavlovna McIntyre, KGB informer and wedding shower planner: I am liked, therefore I am.

"Marina?" Ted tapped on the bedroom door, at the same time opening it. My papers blew off the bed.

On wedding shower day, Donna arrived early with what she called her "effects" and the deep suspicion that I might sneak in some balloons and crepe paper. The silver cardboard bells I had Ted hang up over entryway to dining room before he went to work. Donna reached up her fat thumb and rubbed the silvery foil. "These have HCV," she said.

"What?" I said, coming from the kitchen with a basket of plums and kumquats, mixed. "You know, Donna, until today I thought a kumquat was same thing as an ottoman. We need VCR, did you say?"

"No, HCV. High Camp Value."

"What about crepe paper? I really—"

"*Nyet*, Marina."

I tried to point out that Valeria might *like* the balloons and crepe paper. "Valeria is not Yves Saint Laurent," I said.

"No, but I am," said Donna.

So much I wanted to say, "Yeah, but who's getting married, Yves?"

The whole morning I spent cleaning my good dishes and laying them out. Now she was replacing them with triangles of some space-age-looking plastic. Fruit was dumped from my handwoven baskets into huge white plastic seashells. With the tip of her tongue on her upper lip, she began piling beets on a stone pedestal. They looked like croquet balls.

"No one will just sit down and gnaw beets," I said. This was looking less like food and more like architecture.

"No, but they work." She moved my lamps around so the table was backlit. "The apartment looks great, Marina," she added. She pulled what looked like a rearview mirror off a car door out of her purse. I couldn't imagine what. She took a jar of Beluga caviar from the center of table and dumped it on the mirror. If Doug was anything like this Donna, Valeria was marrying into a family of lunatics.

Putting on my dress for the party, waiting for Ted to come home from work and run the vacuum cleaner (this is his favorite job; he says he gets therapy from it), I prayed that no one from department of Slavic Languages would come. I don't mean pray as euphemism for hope. I said Dear God right up to our cottage-cheese ceiling. *Dear God, please keep them away from our little, cluttered apartment, this silly purple and orange buffet with parts of used cars as serving plates.* I was nervous, like a little child. This was the first party I had hosted in America, even though I had been here almost three years.

Of course, by nine o'clock, when not one person from Slavic had arrived, I was livid. As I welcomed Doug's friends, took their jackets, and asked what they wanted to drink, I thought: Does God only answer prayers for things it turns out you don't really want? Does he only do this to Russians (Dear God, these czars are the pits; what else can you do for us?)? Only to KGB informers? Does he do it to keep you from praying indiscriminately? Then a real horrible thought: Maybe all these prayers addressed to ceilings, prayers prayed all over the world since people started having roofs over their heads, maybe these prayers were answered by ceilings. In which case, what could you expect?

There was not one person here I knew, besides Ted, not one assistant professor or language teacher. Not Bella Semyonovna, not Tanya Olyanovna. Not even Vera, Slavic Department chairman. She was supposedly in Kiev at a conference, but I was mad at her anyway. My stomach was sour. Ted was drinking too much and starting to talk in his fake Russian accent.

People orbited the buffet table. I policed it. I had my orders from Donna: no one could touch until Valeria and Doug arrived. Women with big handbags kept whirling around to hug one another and knocking the beets off the pedestal.

Donna had taken Doug and Valeria out for drinks at seven and they were supposed to be here by eight. I turned my watch to look at it so often that my wrist was getting red.

Finally, at nine-ten, Claire showed up. She had with her a huge present from Bella and Tanya, wrapped elaborately by Bella with several ribbons, and a plastic wedding bell tied up in the bow.

"Is there anything inside, or is wrapping job the present?" I asked. This was petty, not even truly mean. Mean is big, resolute, a Doberman pinscher. Petty is a stupid terrier that bites your pants but not your leg. Claire laughed. She said Bella and Tanya couldn't make it because they were working.

"They sure caught on about America fast," I said, pouring out for Claire a piña colada from the blender. I was getting worse, but I couldn't stop. I was so nervous. "No one would ever give working as excuse in Soviet Union."

"Tanya's doing stand-in stuff on that sitcom about the two sisters. They're shooting tonight, I guess. She should be *in* the show, but her accent kills her. I don't know why they can't just write her in as a neighbor. It's supposed to take place in San Francisco. There aren't any Russians in San Francisco?" I did not want to hear it. I did not want to hear why people weren't here. I knew why people weren't here.

I am KGB! Who knows, there might be hidden microphones in my apartment, cameras peeping out from a basket full of fruit (or, in this case, white plastic seashells full of fruit), other KGB agents. I wanted to call each and every one of those deadbeat Slavists and say, "There is just me, Marina Pavlovna, no devices, no other spies. Come and celebrate Valeria's wedding."

Our tiny air conditioner shivered and dripped. People began stealing food and rearranging it, so I wouldn't see what was gone. At nine-thirty, still no Valeria and Doug. I walked around, telling people not to worry, Doug and Valeria were on their way. No one seemed to care.

Ted was entertaining a gang by the stereo. Several centuries ago, I had asked him to please wait with music until Valeria arrived. How else could we hear Donna's car and hide for the Big Surprise? But the law of parties is the same as the law of thermodynamics: everything goes toward disorder. Music sneaks on. Wine gets spilled on the rug. Your husband's fake Russian accent starts bordering on offensive. He calls you darlink and licks your ear in front of people.

Two of the women standing with Ted had squares of film negative dangling from their pierced ears. Each negative was a picture of a huge diamond earring. They held their hair back with sunglasses and had no hips. Ted introduced them. He said they had started a business called Greek Messengers, where you could hire someone to break bad news to someone else.

"Sort of a more advanced form of singing telegram," said one of them.

"You must be friends of Donna's," I said.

Yes, they said; we were just talking about what we were all doing the summer of "Cinnamon Girl."

Standing with these two, my one bad eardrum booming to the music, watching them show how when they were fifteen and first got stoned but weren't really stoned, they only pretended to be stoned, showing Ted and me and some other, quiet man what a not-stoned fifteen-year-old trying to pretend like she's stoned looks like, a clot of tears rose in my throat.

Like someone slowly wrapping me in a blanket, I realized that Donna and Valeria and Doug weren't coming either. As the darling Greek Messengers wobbled around with lowered eyelids, knocking into Ted's chest and giggling insanely, I saw myself as my cottage-cheese-ceiling God saw me: a foreign woman among forty foreign strangers. I saw this woman smile at an idiotic anecdote recited in a foreign language. I saw her well-meaning but thoroughly foreign husband chortle and hoo hoo! up at the ceiling. I saw a woman coming apart under the secrets she was forced to keep. A woman who had sold her soul to the devil and was now trying to get out of it by having good manners and giving a party.

"Ted," I said, "Ted, could we—I need to ask you."

"Most certainly, darlink. Please, to make an excuse for one moment, please, thank you." He bowed like a German to the Greek Messengers. They laughed tiredly.

I dragged him next to the most heated-up conversation I could find, something about Iran and who'll drop the bomb first.

There were three men pointing at each other with crackers and saying Bullshit. Caviar dribbled off the crackers and onto their shoes.

"Where are they?" I said to Ted. "It's ten o'clock. They were supposed to be here at eight."

"They'll be here," he said, rubbing the sides of my shoulders. "Aren't Russians notorious for being late?"

"Donna is not Russian. I do not think they are coming."

Ted looked down at me. He is big, with good bones, and truly sweet. He loves me. I wanted to brain him. I wanted to wipe that good Ted smile off his big jaw. I wanted to say, "Ted, listen! They are not here because they are afraid of me! They are not here because I am KGB!" Instead I said, whimpering almost, "Maybe a car accident."

"Honey, look, people are having a great time. They'll get here. At least everyone isn't sitting around staring at each other."

"All right." What could I do?

"Can I get you a drink?"

"All right." I stood with my arms dangling at my sides. I was aware I looked like a war victim and not a hostess. The conversation next to me had escalated into nonsense: Who was more terrifying? Soviet Union? Iran? Wait until India gets the bomb. India has the bomb. No it doesn't. Yes it does. Their necks were red from yelling. It was hot in here. It was ten-thirty.

Suddenly, miraculously, there was a breeze. The front door was opening. Cool air and the heavy scent of some California night blossom drifted in.

Then, in came Donna, then Doug, then Valeria. Valeria's eyes were puffy. Her arms were folded. Doug had a splotch of something on his wrinkled pink shirt, which had been made worse by rubbing with water. He looked embarrassed. Donna looked fed up. No one looked surprised. A voice from by the buffet table said, "I thought we were supposed to hide."

I sought Ted's eyes across the room. He was pouring me a vodka. He smiled and toasted me. See, said his American self-assurance, nothing to worry about.

Donna raised her arms dramatically, like a television preacher. "Oi vey!" She seemed to fill half the apartment. Her arms seemed long enough to collect all of us into her embrace. Her bracelets crashed together. "What I do for my brother's happiness! I need a drink." She started for the kitchen, leaving Doug and Valeria at the door.

"I thought you were murdered, or an accident." I trailed behind her. I should have stopped right then. I should have patted her fat shoulder and said, I'm glad you made it. I was worried, but I'm glad you made it. But things must be played out. All cowards and KGB informers and Russian mystics and women who deceive their husbands know this.

I said, "What happened?"

I knew what happened.

Donna turned to me, a wedge of blackberry-carrot cake between her fingers. "Valeria thinks you're a KGB agent. She wouldn't come. I said, 'Honey, this isn't *The Man from U.N.C.L.E.*, it's a goddamn wedding shower.' This is good cake."

I felt Ted's eyes on me. A few people standing around us laughed. One of them said, "I'm a CIA agent; we ought to do lunch sometime." Another one said, "My name's Bond, James Bond." Everything was a joke to this crowd. I *do* work for the people who send people to gulag! India *does* have the bomb!

The phone rang. Out of the corner of my eye, I could see Ted stare at me. When he's not laughing, Ted's eyes are frightening. They become the gray stone eyes of some prehistoric animal that lived in cold water. He went to answer it.

Valeria had joined me at the table. She picked up a paper plate, a special color of plate called Black Cherry that I had to go to several paper-supply stores to find. She was indignant. "That Donna is fruit-cake," she said. "I never said those things." I could tell she had, but I didn't care.

I would care, of course, and I knew I would care. I would care in five minutes, in an hour. I would wish I could take back not caring. I would wish I had made a big scene, that I screamed at her, You and your Russian paranoia practically ruined my party! I cleaned the bathroom for you! You hurt me! But at that instant I was glad to be standing with my fellow Soviet émigré, my officemate and co-worker, deciding what to fill our plates with.

"I like those bells," she said, suddenly. She pointed up at the silver wedding bells above the entryway.

"You do? Someone said they were Ozzie and Harriet. Do you find them Ozzie and Harriet?"

"What is it, Ozzie and Harriet?"

"I don't know."

We laughed.

Ted came then and put a hand on my neck. I didn't turn. The pressure said it all. His long, cold middle finger pressed into the spot between my collarbones. "Telephone," he said. "Your *cousin.*"

"Tell him later, please," I said primly.

"I think you should talk to him now."

"I said later. Valerichka, try this salmon. Flown down from Portland, Oregon, just for your party."

Ted huffed off, as angry and hurt as anyone so
even-tempered can be. He could have, he should have
broken some furniture, or my nose. I on purpose suggested Valeria try some salmon at that very moment
to make it worse. To ruin Ted's illusions completely.
So much for wonderful Russians!

After the party I would sob. I would say I was
quitting KGB. It occurred to me that might be impossible to do, like quitting being pregnant, but anyway . . . I would say I loved him. I do love him. I
would ask forgiveness.

But now . . . well. I took one of those ridiculous
beets and bit into it. Sour earth taste filled my mouth.
I knew I was wrong. Absolutely. There was no trying
to see it another way. No considering the strain emigration has put on me. I was wrong and responsible
for being wrong. Then it rose in me like a mushroom
cloud, pure and horrible: the guilt. Perfect and deep,
the guilt.

I smiled.

# COMMUNIST DOGS

## VERA OMULCHENKO

So. It's Serge and Claire. Serge, my ex-lover. Claire, my secretary. It seems impossible, doesn't it? An exhausted modern cliché. My ex-lover, my secretary. The realization, strapped into the life jacket of logic, refuses to sink in.

Serge is Russian. Not of Russian extraction, as I am, but Moscow born and bred. He's an émigré, a writer, in fact *the* Soviet satirist of his generation, author of the famous *Don't Say Russian When You Mean Soviet.*

She's suburban Southern Californian, addlebrained and built. An aspiring writer of stage and screen, with naturally curly hair. I won't even mention their ages. It seems impossible, doesn't it, that two people so very different could . . . ?

They are in my office. He slouched in a chair in front of my desk, going over his keynote address. She leaning against the doorjamb, with a bag of Magic Markers she's just bought at the bookstore.

"Guess what? Big Mad shot herself," she says. She takes out a red pen, uncaps it. A dainty sniff. "These come in flavors now. She's all right, though. She was cleaning her little pearl-handled thing and it went off." *Thing*, she says. And she wants to be a writer.

"It was inevitable, Claire," says Serge. "I'm sorry."

She's wearing a miniskirt, stone-washed denim. Her thighs are solid and polished. His gaze goes up and down her long body as though he's watching a vertical tennis match.

"It only nicked her. She's really okay. It got her in the calf. The real meaty part. I read somewhere that your calves are a sort of desert of nerve endings. Same with earlobes. That's how people have pierced ears. But noses! Can you imagine piercing your nose? Oogghhh."

Serge laughs, almost giggles. A man who has seen the inside of a Soviet prison, giggling. And who's Big Mad? A character from *Dynasty?* An Irish setter?

"Are those pens for the name tags? If so, be sure you do them in English and Russian," I say. "Get one of the T.A.s to help if you can't manage the Cyrillic."

Behind my back, Claire calls me the Vera-matic. She chops! She slices! She dices! She's all business.

I *am* all business.

"Okay." She stands there, as though waiting for something else. "Hey, how do you like my new skirt?" she blurts out.

"Yes," says Serge. "I like it very much."

And this *look* passes between them, this raw

thing that makes me flush, sending one of those hot, steam-rolled sensations from the roots of my hair to the tips of my professorial pumps. And I'm just *watching*.

Two days before the conference.

Two days before the arrival of eighteen major émigré writers from four different countries.

Two days before all the grant writing, the overseas telephone calls, the telexes, the offers, negotiations, and promises, the setting of the conference schedule, the securing of translators, the confirming of the auditorium space, the renting of folding chairs, the deliberations regarding floral arrangements, food, programs, publicity, would finally come to fruition.

Serge and Claire. My brain feels bent.

Last week, Serge said he missed me. And like any high school girl, I put myself to sleep that night imagining the most delicious reconciliation.

But I am no high school girl. I am a forty-one-year-old department chair with cellulite and a major literary conference on my hands.


I have on my new red linen blazer, through which I'm perspiring like an honest ax murderer hooked up to a lie detector. Serge is standing me up. It's eight forty-five. He's to kick off the conference at nine. And he is nowhere.

The conference participants stumble in, most of them jet-lagged.

Historian Arkady Pavel, in a shiny blue suit studded with grease spots. He stops in the middle of the lobby, grimaces up at a sculpture suspended under the skylight, a massive Möbius strip of film made from panes of green, turquoise, and red gel.

The caterers speed around him, lugging fifty-pound urns of scalding coffee.

"Welcome, welcome, Arkady Ivanovich!" Kiss-kiss on both cheeks. "That is a special sculpture commissioned just for this building, which is part of the cinema complex. Our Department of Cinema is one of the most prestigious in the country."

He screws up his parched face. The sun shining through the sculpture turns it turquoise. "What about Department of Slavic Languages? Who ever heard of literature conference in California?"

"There are many fine universities in California, Arkady Ivanovich."

"Does Ilya Maminov come today?"

"What would a gathering of émigré writers be without the great Maminov? Did you read *Chaff?* I think it's my favorite."

"Maminov is a self-aggrandizing Trotskyite hooligan," he says. "Where is he?"

"This is Maminov or Vyotsky? Both idiots think the jury still is out on Socialism." Zazi Zamyatin-Wrangle, a walleyed, wheelchair-bound epic poet, rolls up with a cup of coffee thrust between his knees. At seventy-three, he is the eldest and most accomplished exiled Soviet poet of the century. We are lucky to have him. He pats my thigh. "Vera, this place is a palace."

"Yes." Pavel sniffs. "A *movie* palace. Have you seen the seats? People will fall asleep before we even get a chance to speak."

Our student office person, Pencil Neck, is in charge of the book table. He's unloading cartons, when he is accosted by Igor Lizowsky.

Igor has a sheaf of poems, all hand-copied, which he insists on arranging himself. He shoves the

other books into a pile and lays out each sheet indi-
vidually.

"Hey, c'mon, there's gotta be room for the other
stuff," says Pencil Neck.

"This is table for selling of literature, correct?"

"Yeah."

"*That* is not literature! *This* is literature! Here,
you read." He thrusts a sheet into Pencil Neck's big
hand. When he glances at it, Igor demands a quarter.

I grab Claire, who is passing out name tags
and information packets. "Go rescue Pen, would
you? Tell Igor you're my assistant. They listen to
authority."

Today's mini is black jersey, which accentuates
Claire's majestic, round rear end. Even old Zazi is
appreciative. And I think: It *was* just a look between
Serge and Claire, nothing more. I was exhausted that
day. Perhaps just jealous. Perhaps blowing it out of
proportion. I adopt a new attitude there and then:
innocent until caught pawing each other.

A reporter from the *Times* is at my elbow. I mistake him at first for a kid here for High School Re-
cruitment Day, also going on this week. He scratches
flecks of sleep from the corners of his eyes and
yawns. He says he wants Serge. Isn't Serge the big
name to watch?

"This isn't a sports event," I say.

"Whatever," he says.

"Serge will be here shortly. Russians are always
late."

Half-filled Styrofoam cups of coffee start piling
up in the ashtrays. People drift into the auditorium.

Most of the audience are citizens from the local
émigré community, which is as expected. Stout,
wrinkled babushkas smelling of boiled cabbage and

old polyester, clutching trampled first editions. Skinny, pale-complected intellectuals who've stolen away from jobs at gas stations, stereo stores.

It doesn't escape my notice that other than Bella Bogoga, a teaching assistant who is leaving at the end of the semester, the colleagues and students in my *own* department can't make time to be here. And Bella, I suspect, gotten up in an outrageous coral-and-turquoise floral number, is only here to get autographs.

I spot the auburn curls of Claire across the room. She is entertaining Ben Bara Abramovicz in her sub-elementary-school Russian. I ask her to track Serge down. Call him at home. Check the morgue.

I get a perverse pleasure watching her hurry through the crowd to the pay phone, like thrusting my tongue into a cavity. Her strides are long, Amazonian. She is probably the kind of woman who looks better in clothes than out of them. Why is this a relief? I watch her dial. Just as I thought. She knows his number by heart. Either that or she knows the morgue's number by heart.

It's my own fault Serge isn't here.

Two days ago, after Claire sashayed off to her name tags, and Serge and I resumed our discussion on his opening address, I did something I had promised myself I wouldn't.

I told him about Gennady Blizitsky. I don't know why. It was the worst strategy imaginable. The idea of Serge and Claire had me shaken, rattled, rolled. Everything.

I mentioned to Serge a telex I had received that morning from Ludmila Boky. She was backing out of the conference because she suddenly remembered that Zazi Zamyatin-Wrangle had insulted her nineteen years ago.

Serge admonished me, mock serious. "Always remember, Vera, feuding is part of our heritage. Dostoevsky had it in for Turgenev, and Pushkin bit the big one in a duel. Is like gambling, epilepsy, and overwriting—all of us have a tendency for it!"

I laughed. It was a solid, warm moment like the old days. I took advantage of this closeness and confessed that an old, old enemy of his was coming to the conference, which would give him a chance to prove his reasonableness about all this infighting and unnecessary hysteria.

It was the wrong thing to have confessed.

He sputtered and spewed and cursed. He promised me if Gennady Blizitsky set foot anywhere near him, I would regret it.

Years ago, something horrible happened between them. My sources in Moscow were vague, and Serge would never talk about it. They collaborated on *Trespassers Welcome Here*, then somehow Serge went to prison and Gennady got a dacha down the road from Yevtushenko. Then Serge emigrated. Now, surprisingly, Gennady.

I tried to defend myself. My job was to put on a conference bringing together the most well-known Soviet émigré writers of the age. Gennady wrote the famous *Of Three Minds*, a satire about a psychotic Politburo bigwig who had the personalities of a Party member, a dissident, and a professional gymnast. I couldn't very well neglect him, could I, just because Serge said he was a Politburo pimp?

Serge said I knew nothing, *nothing* about Soviet writers. I ordered him out of my office.

With one eye on the door, I listen to Sasha Mikivinsky divulge bits about his new masterpiece-in-progress, *The Perils of Private Peres Troika*. Claire reappears, breathless, chest notably heaving.

Serge is, in fact, already here.

I discover him in the back row of the auditorium, doing a crossword puzzle. "You are dead," I say.

"No, I am protesting. What is six-letter word for jack-of-all-trades?"

"Can't you protest after you give your address? There's someone here from the *Times.*"

"What is a jack-of-all-trades? Like a car jack? A guy always jacking off?" He laughs at his joke.

"Why are you doing this? Haven't you hurt me enough?"

This gets me a look. He takes off his glasses. A wisp of a thought trails through my mind: he looks very middle-aged with his glasses. If he wears them with Claire, she's bound to see this and . . .

"I hurt *you?*" he says. "Don't be absurd. Gennady Blizitsky is an intriguer, a despicable Communist dog. I wouldn't be surprised if he is KGB. How can you expect me to be into a conference which involves this kind of man?"

I rub my eyes. "Serge. For me? Just this once?" It sounds as feeble as it is.

"I am putting together a petition to evacuate him off the conference. You will hear it tomorrow afternoon."

A little-known function of the Vera-matic is Quick Thinking. What can I do? I glance around the auditorium for a replacement.

I need a Russian literary General Patton to send the troops into the conference with confidence, heads held high. Zazi Zamyatin-Wrangle would be the obvious choice, but he's a little on the ponderous side.

A really nasty thing to do would be to get Gennady, and at the same time I'm saying I couldn't *possibly* do that, the better I like the idea. Gennady is a bona fide Slavic sentimentalist, a blond, broad-chested guy who sobs and bangs his head on the table the way other people drum their fingers.

I see him sitting in the front row, caressing his armrests, reveling in the deep red plush of the theater seats.

The interpreters are down by the stage, headphones on, ready to begin. They wear the grim faces you see on men at Mission Control. Riva will do Russian to English for all the English speakers in the audience, Nikolai English-Russian for all the Russian speakers, and Stu is backup. They are getting paid by the job, not the hour.

All the intellectuals have their headphones already in place; the babushkas have trained their coke-bottle-bottomed glasses on the empty stage.

Suddenly Nikolai speaks. While reading his lips I hear, bleating through four hundred headphones, *"Are we going to get this fucking show on the road?"*

Gasps and giggles slide quickly into the rumbling and mumbling of the discontented. I make a decision.

Gennady doesn't use the mike. He has tears in his throat. A fist, for some reason, over his heart. He talks about how he loves United States, how he loves Russia. He loves the *people* of U.S.A., the *people* of Soviet Union. Nothing about the conference, nothing about literature. He raps his chest for emphasis. He should have been the floor show at the Geneva Accords.

I start thinking I should have gone with the ponderous Zazi, when Claire appears at the back of the auditorium, pushing a battered suitcase held together with electrical tape. Down the aisle she goes. Her skirt hikes up dangerously in the back.

Gennady must have sent her back to the Hilton

to retrieve his papers. Asked at the last minute to fill in for the keynote speaker, he couldn't have been expected to come up with something profound and erudite off the top of his head. I settle back in my seat.

Gennady unwinds the tape, pops open the suitcase.

Maminov and Vyotsky, both in the front row, tip out of their seats and peak inside.

Claire looks confused. "Dirt?"

Dirt?

"Earth!" shouts Gennady. "Russian earth! Brought out of Soviet Union with me." He picks up a crumbling rock in each hand. "Is for you. My old people. My new people!" He bends down on one knee, arms outstretched toward the front row, gray crumbs trickling from between his fingers onto the carpet.

The audience is stiff and unsure.

But Claire, Claire the artless, Claire the ingenuous, Claire the gal with the gaga gams, punctures this tight, awkward moment. She smiles out at us blindly, puts her palm out to Gennady. "You never know when you might want to break a window. I mean, dirt clods are good for something."

Vyotsky hops up after her. And soon every Russian in the auditorium *must* have his own hunk of Russian soil. It's like Eucharist at a sod outlet. People are orderly and reverential. Some of the more nostalgic bury their noses in their dry, hard handfuls, redolent not of Mother Russia but of the inside of Gennady's suitcase. Bella Bogoga wraps her chunk carefully in an orange scarf taken from around her neck and deposits it in her purse. Igor Lizowsky is in tears. Even the reporter for the *Times* goes up. He takes a picture.

Serge grabs me by the arm. He is shaking, his

swarthy square face gone gray. "This is the worst kind of Slavic schmaltz imaginable!"

"It's all right," I say. "The audience loves it. It's a good way to start."

" 'The audience loves it'! You sound like a producer!"

"You mean like a film producer? What do you know about film producers, Sergei Pavlovich?" I know what he knows. He knows what Claire, aspiring writer of stage and screen, tells him. Confesses to him. Late at night. Her strong Californian sleekness wrapped in his burly Russian arms.

During our midmorning coffee break on the second day, the news comes, a woman reporter with a TV-cameraman in tow. This morning in the *Times*, there was Gennady and his Russian earth, with the caption "Wild and crazy guy wows 'em at local lit meet." Nothing about the conference, or the reason Gennady had dragged a suitcase full of soil halfway around the world.

I intercept them by the glazed donuts. "You're here to cover the conference?"

"It's human interest," says the reporter, a blonde with straight black eyebrows and a wincing smile. "Where's the guy with the dirt clods?"

"That was yesterday," I say. "This afternoon he's on a panel discussing the influence of neo-Stalinism on third-wave émigré writing."

"If Gennady Ilyich is human interest, are other American news items nonhuman or inhuman?" Valeria Chalisian-Pendell asks the cameraman. Valeria is another teaching assistant, helping out with the coffee.

"I don't know. Last week we went out to some county fair and did a story on these pigs who've been trained to race through this huge maze thing. You know what's at the end of the maze? An Oreo in a pie tin."

"Oh," says Valeria.

"I don't think you'll find our conference that exciting," I say.

"So what's the appeal of Russian earth?" asks the reporter. "And do we know, was it *real* Russian earth? How do we know he didn't load up his suitcase outside?" She gestures through the glass doors of the auditorium to a gardener putting in some marigolds.

"Let me just introduce you to Gennady," I say, leading the reporter over to the book table, where Gennady is autographing copies of *Of Three Minds.*

Our small procession does not go unnoticed, particularly by the writers. All the talk since yesterday has been about how Gennady's books are suddenly selling.

"By the way," I say, "in your story could you mention that this is the first conference of its kind, bringing together the most well-known Soviet émigré writers in the world?"

"Sure," she says.

"Tomorrow we're going to hold a special panel discussion on Solzhenitsyn. If you have time to mention that."

"Solzhenitsyn's here? Can we get him and this Gennady both with dirt clods?"

"No, no, Solzhenitsyn's not here. This is a panel, discussing his rabid Russophilism. Also, Ilya Maminov is going to speak on the role of fantasy and satire in the explication of Soviet political realities."

"Wow, sounds great."

"Don't you want to write this down, or . . . or film me or something?"

"I'll remember. Say, could we get Gennady outside by that planter?"

"Of course. Perhaps we can get a pile of his
books. Maybe some of the other writers too."

"No, just him. Mr. Gennady! Hello, I'm Kelly
Campbell from Channel Five News!"

"Hello!" says Gennady. He gestures with a book.
"Vera, give a telephone call to Chicago to my pub-
lishers. We are running out!"

"Will do," I say. Then, pulling the reporter aside
for a moment: "Ms. Campbell, you won't quote me
on the rabid Russophilism, will you? I mean, I
wouldn't want to do anything to sour Solzhenitsyn's
reputation among your viewers."

"Hey," she says, "don't worry."

That afternoon, when Serge is finally ready to
present his petition, the auditorium is filled to ca-
pacity.

Everyone is here to be wowed, I presume, to
watch the wild and crazy in action. Students lean
against the back wall, book bags hanging off their
shoulders. Professors and university staff peek in
from time to time.

Still, I think, is that so bad? Attendance is attendance. Maybe among all the curiosity seekers there
is actually someone who reads.

Serge goes to the podium. He dismisses the interpreters, preferring to do his own translation.

He clears his throat and begins.

First it's writing. It's about what it is to be a
writer. About a writer's responsibility to the people
and not the regime, about the insidious effects of
writing for approval in any society, but especially a
totalitarian one. And then Gennady: Gennady's history, Gennady's talents and shortcomings as a writer,

Gennady's recanting during the *Trespassers Welcome Here* period. And somehow, suddenly, seamlessly, he's got Malraux and Martin Luther King and Simone de Beauvoir in there, he's got Lillian Hellman refusing to cut her conscience to fit this year's fashion, and Camus quoted in the original French, translated perfectly into Russian, then perfectly into English, and he intimates, he practically *proves*, they'd all be supporting him if they were here, they'd all be saying that Gennady Blizitsky, who, in the past, so compromised his work for the sake of silk shirts and a dacha and tickets to hockey games and an internal passport, should not be allowed to sit with the great exiled Soviet writers who have suffered and are with us today, and the list of these great writers gets read—Arkady Pavel, Andrei Sinyavsky—and Serge's voice is deep and strident, without a trace of his usual self-effacing humor—Zazi Zamyatin-Wrangle, Iosef Brodsky—and the spit hisses and bubbles on his lips—Viktor Nekrasov, Ben Bara Abramovicz— and I'm staring at him, deeply moved, hypnotized, lulled by the importance, the weight of the names, and suddenly I'm remembering Serge in Moscow before he emigrated, I'm remembering a heavier man, a feverish, drunken man, shirtless even though it was March, sweating like a coal miner in his tiny apartment, which was no more than a corridor with doors on either end, and he had just gotten out of jail and was nevertheless launching some new protest, and he was laughing and his eyes were boiling bright slits and he was saying, "My brain is flammable! Ideas are matches!" and I'm thinking it was true then, and it's true now, and all my sadness, my regret that it's over between us, disappears and I feel honored and privileged just to have had the opportunity to know this brilliant, passionate person, and when he ends, quietly, with his own name, I'm weeping and I'm applauding.

Then, out of the corner of my eye, I see someone yawning. Yawning and leaving. Leaving in that sneaky, don't-notice-me way, head down. I'm stunned. This has been the high point of the conference. Someone is *walking out?* I turn around in my seat and see that the auditorium is half empty.

The man sitting next to me, a professor of political science, snores gently.

Suddenly Gennady leaps out of his seat, startling us both. "What, Sergei Pavlovich, is a Communist dog?"

"What?" Serge fumbles, replacing his reading glasses in their case. He's distracted, drained.

"You accused me of being a Communist dog. What is it? We all know Soviet Union is a *Socialist* state."

"You. I. You know." Serge stares at him, anger pushing blood into his face.

"Oh, yes! Yes!" Gennady nods his head, drums his upper lip with his fingers. "I think I've *had* one. It comes with chili, red caviar, and onions, right?"

The few people still paying attention laugh.

At dinner, Serge fumes and rails, rails and fumes. We have closed a local Russian restaurant especially for the conference. It is our big night. There is a Russian band, Stolichnaya.

He sits alone with a bottle, won't touch the cold sturgeon in aspic, one of his favorite dishes. He won't dance. Even Zazi Zamyatin-Wrangle participates, pulling Claire out on the floor and twirling around her in his wheelchair.

"It was beautiful," I say.

"It was boring. I don't have any cheap theatrics

in my sleeve, so no one is interested. Thought is an enema to this country!"

A giggle slips out. "You mean anathema, don't you?"

"Don't you laugh at me too!"

"I'm not laughing. Serge, listen, I'm not laughing." He lets me rub his arm. Feeling the tweed under my fingers, I remember that other worry. I'm a little drunk myself, so I ask, "Serge, are you . . . have you got someone new? A new . . . a girlfriend?"

"No. Yes." He stares straight ahead. I don't have to look to know that at the end of straight ahead is Claire.

"That's what I thought," I say, forcing myself to laugh like a friend.

"You know the saying 'on again, off again'? This one's off again, off again."

"So it's over, or what?"

"No, it is one of those that will never be over, even when it's over."

"I know about that." I touch his neck.

"Gennady Blizitsky!" Serge slams his glass on the table. "He is a hack. He makes jokes about his collusion with those Supreme Soviet shits. 'What is a Communist dog?' No sense of responsibility, no remorse. And now everyone is buying his books! Is disgusting."

Eating and drinking so much so late gives me harrowing dreams. The conference has literally turned into a circus: Anna Khotochevko wheels up and down the aisles on a unicycle; Maminov, his face painted, tosses around a pair of flaming Indian clubs; and Claire and Serge make love under the book table, to the accompaniment of calliope music.

Today is the final day, and our program is full.

In the morning, there are two panels and two readings; in the afternoon, Gennady has asked for time to present his own petition.

A young woman is waiting for me when I come to open up the auditorium. "Hiya, what's going on? I'm Suki from *People.*"

"Nothing. This is a conference on Soviet émigré writing. I doubt your readers would be interested. Excuse me."

"No, no! This is the place!" It's Serge. His hair is still wet and curling around his ears. He's in the best mood I've seen him in in seven years. He charms Suki from *People* with a comedic retelling of how yesterday, without the aid of artificial depressants or a six-hour Andy Warhol movie, he put half the people in the country interested in émigré literature to sleep. "Stick around today; it will be entertaining, I assure you." He winks.

"Claire won't be here until later," he tells me.

I immediately think she's recovering from a night of love, which also accounts for his terrific mood. "She'd better get here soon. And don't wink at reporters."

"Did I wink? Why would I wink?" He winks first one eye, then the other.

"Don't," I say. "Behave yourself, all right? You gave your petition; now just calm down."

I'm furious at Claire. *She* couldn't call me? *He* had to tell me? I need her.

Someone needs to adjust the mike for Zazi; we're out of coffee, we need to order more potato salad for lunch; someone needs to call Campus Security to break up a fight between Arkady Pavel and Ilya Maminov, which, I suspect, has been staged completely for the benefit of the infernal reporters, the omnipresent cameras.

After lunch, Serge disappears, and what happens is as bad as anything I could have imagined. No, worse. I couldn't have imagined this. Because I am a scholar. An administrator. My Vera-matic capabilities only extend to getting grants in on time, putting on conferences to further the appreciation of literature.

As Gennady stands, shuffles his papers at the podium, I swear I hear sniffing and scratching. The soft tearing of toenails on carpet. I turn and look around. The doors leading from the auditorium into the lobby are closed. Nothing.

Now, how Serge could *know* that Gennady would open his rebuttal with "What is a Communist dog?" is beyond me. Did he steal his petition from his hotel room? Or is it just one of those things floating around in the collective unconscious of all these lackeys, hoodlums, provocateurs, tools, and renegades?

"What," begins Gennady, "is—a Communist— dog?"

At that moment, the doors fly open and hundreds of red dogs bolt into the auditorium. Those who love dogs laugh and reach out for them; those who hate them scream and shrink back.

It seems like hundreds. Actually, there are only five. And they are not really red at all, but sort of a half-assed henna. They are big dogs, retriever types, with long, rolling pink tongues. They lope up and down the aisles, sniffing and peeing and scratching and licking and wagging their bodies like mad.

As though on cue, one collie-looking dog bolts up on stage and thrusts his long nose into Gennady's crotch. Gennady yelps and tries to shoo him away with his petition.

At the back of the auditorium, Serge howls and

yells, "Communist dogs!" Everyone with a camera is taking his picture.

Claire is hiding in the lobby.

"What is this?" I shout at her. "Are you out of your fucking mind?"

"I'm sorry. I know you're mad. It's just—well, I'm quitting anyway. I know you're going to fire me. I need to quit anyway, to do my writing."

"You bet I'm going to fire you." I listen for the sounds of snapping teeth, for some old voice bellowing in Russian that it's going to sue me. "Whose idea was it, yours or his?"

"Well, sort of both of ours. You know, he was pretty depressed last night, and I said—"

"I *don't* want to know."

"Look, the dogs belong to my aunt out in Sylmar. She's a crazy dog lady. That's where I was all morning, driving out there. They're all good dogs, they're all trained."

From inside, laughing. Doggy mooing, people cooing.

Serge bursts out of the auditorium, rubbing his hands. "Order more books!"

"The conference ends in four hours," I say, feeling like a wet blanket.

He throws his arms around Claire. A comfortable old gesture. I suddenly understand how long this has been going on with them. I must have been too busy putting together the conference to even notice. "Success!" he says. "You are beautiful!"

"Ser-urge." She wriggles away from him, embarrassed in front of me.

"Did you like the red?" Serge asks me.

"It's hair junk, I use it on my own hair. I mean, it rinses out; it won't hurt the dogs or anything," says Claire.

"Oh, good. I was worried about the dogs," I say.

I go and prop open the doors of the auditorium. All the dogs skitter out except the collie, who is still down on stage, kissing and sniffing Gennady.

Before I call the conference to order and give Gennady a chance to continue if he wants to, I look back and see the sun shining through the film sculpture on a turquoise Serge, a green Claire, laughing, surrounded by red Communist dogs pursuing scents in the carpet.